While jaggedly comical and charming, Dave Madden's fiction is a sharp reflection of our darker moods, a rich skewering of domestic life, of workplace perversities, of misguided therapy. These portraits of families, lovers, and friends are smart, moving, and funny.

Timothy Schaffert, author of *The Swan Gondola: A Novel*

This is a fiction debut brimming with wisdom and wit where characters are forced into the periphery of their own lives and struggle to overcome the impediments they pose to their own happiness. Dave Madden renders these characters with the fond and exacting accuracy of a mathematician plying a notoriously unsolvable problem. These are people who might have given in to desperation were it not so impractical and who live with a moving fastidiousness of spirit in an effort to overcome "the chasms and imbalances we create."

Kellie Wells, author of *Fat Girl, Terrestrial: A Novel*

Dave Madden has again given us a wonder of a book. These charismatic stories, as funny as they are sad, are attuned to the possibility of disorder beneath every human aspiration.

Paul Lisicky, author of *The Narrow Door*

A wry, deliciously smart sensibility presides over the magnificently multi-tentacled *If You Need Me I'll Be Over There*. The title story alone is worth the price of admission, delivering the book to a place of exquisite, wondrous tenderness. Dave Madden is a protean talent and his story collection is a treasure trove.

Maud Casey, author of *The Man Who Walked Away*

If You Need Me I'll Be Over There

break away books

MICHAEL MARTONE

IF
YOU
NEED
ME
I'LL
BE
OVER
THERE

Dave Madden

Indiana University Press
Bloomington & Indianapolis

This book is a publication of

Indiana University Press
Office of Scholarly Publishing
Herman B Wells Library 350
1320 East 10th Street
Bloomington, Indiana 47405 USA

iupress.indiana.edu

The paper used in this publication
meets the minimum requirements of
the American National Standard for
Information Sciences—Permanence
of Paper for Printed Library
Materials, ANSI Z39.48–1992.

Manufactured in the
United States of America

Library of Congress
Cataloging-in-Publication Data

Madden, Dave, [date]
    [Short stories. Selections]
    If you need me I'll be over there /
Dave Madden.
    pages cm. — (Break away books)
    ISBN 978-0-253-02062-8 (print :
alk. paper) — ISBN 978-0-253-02071-0
(e-book)
    I. Title.
    PS3613.A2834685 A6
    813'.6—dc23

                              2015032071

1 2 3 4 5   21 20 19 18 17 16

For Neal

"Crawling at your feet," said the Gnat (Alice drew her feet back in some alarm), "you may observe a Bread-and-butter-fly. Its wings are thin slices of bread-and-butter, its body is a crust, and its head is a lump of sugar."

"And what does *it* live on?"

"Weak tea with cream in it."

A new difficulty came into Alice's head. "Supposing it couldn't find any?" she suggested.

"Then it would die, of course."

"But that must happen very often," Alice remarked thoughtfully.

"It always happens," said the Gnat.

LEWIS CARROLL, *Through the Looking-Glass*

Contents

Acknowledgments

Previous versions of stories in this collection appeared in *Barrelhouse, Beloit Fiction Journal, Hawai'i Review, HOBART, Indiana Review, New Ohio Review,* and *Prairie Schooner.* I'm grateful to the editors of those journals for their early encouragement. Also many thanks are due to the following people for their help in putting this book together: Jonis Agee, Chris Arnold, Ryan Call, Elizabeth Conner, Jim Gavin, Donal Godfrey, Heather Streckfus-Green, Tyrone Jaeger, Jesse Lee Kercheval, Ebonie Ledbetter, Pam and Ted Madden, Shani Madden, Michael Martone, Tim O'Brien, Adam Peterson, Christine Schutt, Jim Scott, Jim Shepard, Judy Slater, Nathan Walters, and Jenny Ward. I owe Sarah Jacobi much gratitude for taking a chance on this book and even more to Gail Hochman and Jody Kahn for their ongoing support of my work. And finally, thanks to Neal Nuttbrock—a dedication isn't enough to say how much I love you.

If You Need Me I'll Be Over There

Pamela

MY DAD BOUGHT ME A CAR AND HE WOULDN'T LET ME touch it until I could type sixty words a minute, because he said that computers were the wave of the future. This was back when saying that sort of thing still sounded prophetic, back when *responsibility* was only a word I'd hear now and again on the radio, so I didn't have any means of arguing with him. "Fine," I said. "What kind of car is it?"

"Alfa Romeo," he said. He stood tall in my doorway, wearing high shorts and a T-shirt with holes around the collar, the keys dangling from the dealership's complimentary keychain. "You can looky but no touchy."

I went outside and lookied. Charcoal grey. Black ragtop. I stood in front of it at the head of our driveway with my hands on my hips like I used to when I was a little girl bossing boys around the grade school's blacktop, and the Romeo looked like a face that was grinning as it met me for the first time. *Hello, there.* We eyeballed one another and I did the math, and we came to the conclusion that pecking out one word a second couldn't be that difficult. I would be driving this car by the end of the month.

In the meantime, she needed a name.

"What about Romeo?" Bridget said.

I held the phone away from my head and looked at it in wild disbelief. "That's a boy's name and this car is a lady. A Beautiful Lady. She deserves a beautiful name."

Bridget was a natural blonde. Her curls hung off her head like fern fronds. Of the two of us, I was the creative one, but still I gave her a month to come up with something perfect. Now we both had projects to get us through to college.

The next day my dad and I drove to the mall in Mission Viejo to find some typing software compatible with our Apple IIe. I asked why we couldn't take my car. "If you can find a way to ride without touching it, sweetheart, I'll be glad to," he said. So I sat in his boring Lincoln, slouched the whole way there, trying to envision what the wide California sky would look like over our heads. At the computer store they had not one but two programs that taught Apple IIe users to type, each with a cartoony guide.

"Which do you like?" my dad asked. "The donkey or the cobra?"

"Aren't donkeys slow?" I asked. I needed speed and I needed it soon and I didn't want any impediments.

"Erica, just pick one."

I picked the cobra. It was my boyfriend's favorite snake. At least I thought it was. When we got home I called him and let him know a computer cobra would be teaching me to type, and he said, "Sweet. Did they have a python?"

"No," I said. "Just a donkey and a cobra."

"A python would've been sweet."

I didn't have a response for this, so I let the line go silent for a bit and played at a kink in the phone cord. "I'm sad," I said after a while.

"Huh?" he said. "Why?"

"I'm sad you're going to be gone so long." He was leaving the next day on a monthlong Outward Bound trip.

"Aw, babe, I'll be back soon. It's like . . . twenty-eight days. Or twenty-nine, with travel."

All those days lined up in a row somehow made it worse, made the time seem longer than one simple month standing all alone. "Can't I come see you tonight?"

"I gotta leave at six in the morning," he said. "My mom won't let you."

I breathed slowly and deeply so I wouldn't end up crying. My mom would've let you, I wanted to say, but instead I told him I loved him and hung up the phone, picturing a python strangling his mother at the neck. *Attack!* Then I pictured her struggling in the backseat of my new car, my boyfriend and me laughing up front with the wind ribboning our hair and the sun beating down on us like hellfire.

That night after dinner my dad installed the software and I got to work. I'd used computers before but never in a timed setting. Never under pressure. When it started, the cobra told me his name was Conrad and then asked me what my name was. So I started typing.

e-r-i-c-a

Then Conrad introduced me to the shift key and asked for my name again.

EEEEE

I wasn't going to relinquish control this early.

Greetingsssss, EEEEE! he said, like a cobra would if it could talk, and I slowly learned about the home row, irritated that it included the semicolon because I had no intentions of using the thing. Just as well that it sat under my right pinky as I had no intentions of using that, either. The first thing I learned as Conrad fed me banal sentences about regular exercise and floppy diskettes is that typing took four eyes, or at least a keen third. Because I couldn't see the screen and the keys at the same time, I had to move my head a lot, and as I typed I felt like some Japanese businessman bowing emphatically at everything Conrad was saying. By the time I was done with the first round, my neck was tight and squashed like putty. He calculated my score and it was twenty-two words per minute. Not even half. So I went on to round two with the clever plan to hit the keys as fast as I could, but Conrad was cleverer. He didn't let me advance in the sentence until I backspaced and corrected mistypes. End of round two: seven. Conrad deducted wpm for each error.

Enough. I escaped Conrad and his program and went to the den to watch *Knots Landing.* My dad was there nodding off in his La-Z-Boy, his hand cradling a dewy tumbler of something on ice. I woke him up by mussing his hair and he pulled sharply away from me. "You're serious about this typing thing?" I asked.

"Sure am," he said, rousing and shifting his heft around. "I've got to look out for your future. What kind of job can you expect to get with no typing ability? Shopgirl? Streetwalker?"

I rolled my eyes and tutted my tongue, playing the part of a teenager. "Wasn't mom a shopgirl?"

"That was a different time. You can be anything. What do you want to be?"

I sat next to him on the floor and wetted a thumb along his glass and then tried to write my name in the chair's leather. I got to *i* before my thumb went dry. "I'm waiting for it to come to me. Like I'll be driving down the street—in the car, of course—and I'll see a billboard that'll click. Or I'll take some class to fulfill a requirement and the professor will say something very profound sometime in the third or fourth week, something about the cosmos, maybe, and he'll be looking at me when he says it and I'll just know."

Now it was Dad's turn to roll his eyes. "It never happens that way," he said, raising the lever next to me and lifting himself out of his chair. "You'll see."

I said good night and sat there on the floor staring at the television, and I wondered how many words, exactly. How many would I have to type tomorrow, and the next day, and the next until I'd get to sixty a minute? And then thereafter, how many words did I have yet to type before I died quietly in my nineties? Millions? Trillions? Given what they said about monkeys and Shakespeare, I knew it was probable that I could type out enough words in the right order to really impress someone someday, but would that someone ever be me? If my future was meant to be tied to a machine, I wanted it to be tied to a car, to something mobile and fast, and not something that offered only keys with letters printed on them against which I could press my fingers millions of billions of times. Even if I became a writer, even if I chose art over wealth, I would write by longhand. That night in bed, I promised myself this before falling fitfully asleep.

Bridget called later that week with her first idea. "What about Connie?"

I was drinking a grapefruit-juice spritzer and nearly spit it out. "Oh my god, that's so weird that's almost the name of the snake on my program."

"The what?"

I explained the situation and asked her how she knew.

"I didn't," she said. "I just thought it would go well with the car."

"Well, try again." Connie was the name of some nebbishy woman from the 1950s, some head of the town's temperance league.

That wasn't my car. I wanted my car to be more subdued, even if it was a showy Alfa Romeo. Even if it would catch the sun in winking glints as I'd speed it around corners. So subdued, but also fierce. Like a cobra.

That day with Conrad was no better than the day before. What he'd do, as I'd type, was slither underneath the words, letter by letter. Then he'd coil up vertically at the end and say something sibilant and encouraging like *Nicccce job!* or *Sssssuper!* And then he'd tell me I was typing in the low twenties, and we'd start all over again. The problem as I saw it was the sentences I had to type. I understood that they were meant to exercise my fingers, force them through habit into certain patterns of motion, but I wasn't the type to divorce myself from reality, and when typing out *The sad fed dog was ready for care,* I had to think, What dog on the planet is *sad* after being fed? What kind of care, psychiatric? That afternoon Conrad told me that *Jill may pick an onion in July,* expecting me to care half as much about this pending decision as Jill must have. "I'll never type that sentence in my *ganze leben,*" I said out loud. "You're being stupid."

And then Conrad's next sentence—*Don't cry, try another voyage*—was so full of cheek I shut the machine off without booting down first.

I called Bridget but she wasn't home, and I wished I could have hung out with my boyfriend, but of course he wasn't home either. He was out in the desert somewhere learning to follow orders. I suppose it was better than the alternative. To spend six months in Juvenile Hall amid a bunch of street thugs and gangbangers would probably put a lot worse strain on your skinny little body than a month of bare-bones hiking and camping would. And James's body was terribly skinny—wrists I could wrap a thumb and pinky around, ill-fitting clothes that hung on his frame like a scarecrow's rags, a butt the size of a blueberry muffin. Maybe when he got back he'd be stronger and thicker, a tough guy. Maybe instead of a pinky I'd need to use my middle finger.

Even before we had graduated from high school Bridget and I had graduated from getting shitfaced at keggers on the beach. Beer made me bloated and gave me an awful time in the bathroom the next morning, whereas wine rose up to my head and nested there like canaries ready to take flight, so for fun we stopped going to other people's parties and started hostessing parties of our own. Tonight it was her turn and we had an odd number of guests because of my boyfriend, and to remedy the punched-gut feeling of his absence I found some paper in the study and drew his face from memory, including the little scar that sliced his left eyebrow in two and the tendrils of hair at the base of his neck that curled up toward the ears. Underneath I wrote "(James)" for clarity and taped it to the back of the chair that should have been his. The empty chair next to mine.

When the doorbell rang, I was shuffling through Bridget's dad's jazz records looking for the one with the blackest man on the cover. I put it on and opened the door and there was everyone, clumped in a mass on the porch.

"We carpooled," Nathan said. "I sat on Robbie's lap." Robbie nodded like a good boy and in filed the Beautiful Prettys—the art-rock combo for which Nathan was drummer—with their silent girlfriends in tow. I handed these girlfriends wine glasses. The boys drank the beer they brought. Bridget came in and kissed Nathan hello and stood right next to him, which was always cute because they were both five-two.

"Well, here we all are," Nathan said, but here we all weren't, because my boyfriend was sweating out his guilt in the middle of the desert. And then he said, "Uh, not James, I suppose."

"He's here in spirit," I said and led us all to the table, pointing out the drawing and demanding everyone say hello.

Bridget served the food restaurant-style, delivering fully plated meals of cauliflower curry with couscous and chutney to the table. "Shouldn't we be having rice with this?" Robbie asked, and Bridget said no we shouldn't be, and conversation commenced from there. Where were Bridget's folks tonight? They were at another restaurant opening. Which one was this? Some Brazilian place out in Irvine, where they brought huge skewers of animal flesh to your table, which obviously was a personal assault on everything Bridget believed in, and she didn't plan on eating another meal of her mother's again, not that she ever cooked. When were the Beautiful Prettys playing next? Some house party in El Toro next weekend. It'd been a slow month. Wouldn't it be great if they could play a wedding? No one they knew was getting married, and this last comment of Nathan's caused enough tension among the couples that we swallowed the conversation along with our bites of Bridget's dinner. Maybe desperation eventually led Bridget to tell everyone I had a new car waiting for me, one I couldn't touch until I learned to type, which rustled up so much stupid boy-commotion that I threw a cardamom pod at her head. Those days we'd say anything just to see what happened next.

"He want you to be a secretary?" Robbie asked. All eyes fell on me. I chewed extra slowly to make them wait.

"He thinks computers are the wave of the future."

"What do you think?" This was Alan, the Beautiful Prettys' vocalist, who once tried to sleep with me and whom I didn't like to look in the eye.

"I don't even know what 'wave of the future' means."

"If computers are the future," Alan said, still staring at me, "then we're all destined to become mindless fucking robots."

By this point everyone was sufficiently bummed out and I saw Bridget elbow Nathan, who disappeared in the kitchen and came out with a tray of cookies. These were his trademark at dinner parties, fortunes written on small pieces of paper and pierced like hors d'oeuvres with fancy toothpicks, which then got implanted into a snickerdoodle, the only cookie he knew how to make. In the end they looked nothing like fortune cookies, but more like flat white ships sailing off to our mouths. We passed the tray like people did at church and each took a cookie. Nathan suggested we read aloud in alphabetical order, so Alan went first: *Three varieties of cheese lie on your path: Roquefort, Limburger, Wensleydale.* Absurdism was Nathan's whole thing. He wrote the lyrics whenever the Beautiful Prettys decided they needed some. Robbie's girlfriend, Amy, spoke up for the first time all night to read hers: *Onward, fighting through the hoar, the dogsled of your deepest hopes is making record time.* Many people sighed in admiration at this. Bridget got the curt one that seemed requisite: *Facsimilate platitudes.*

"I hate this one like I hate you," she told Nathan and balled it up and dropped it in his beer.

Then it was my turn. I picked the paper up with two fingers and pulled the pick out with my teeth, which I pushed over to the side of my mouth like a trucker. I read the thing quickly to myself—*There's a tremor in the timbre of your mother's voice as she calls you in for dinner from the front porch of your current hardship/obstacle.*—and all of a sudden I felt a hard, hot gripping around my heart and lungs.

"I don't want to read mine."

"C'mon," Robbie said. "You have to."

"I don't, actually," I said and left the fortune lying in the last of my chutney.

* * *

Bridget called the next morning and passed the phone to Nathan, who said, "I didn't mean, like, your actual mother. It was a figurative mother. Like a *metaphorical* one. It was the idea: mother. You know?"

I assured him I did and told him what I told everyone when the subject of my mom came up, which was that she'd left when I was so young that I barely had any memory of the woman, and that she'd done such a great job of disappearing that I hadn't the foggiest where she was or what she was like. All this was true. What I didn't say is that her absence still carved an emptiness out of me, opening up dark caverns of wants more painful than My Boyfriend Back and The Keys To My New Car In My Pocket because of their ambiguity, because what in fact *did* I want? My Mother Back wasn't quite it, because I didn't even know my mother and by that point in her life she could have been a terrible person. A Mother Like Everyone Else Has wasn't right either, because I didn't even like most people's mothers. Even now, the closest I can ever get to pinning it down would be Not To Have To Want A Mother In The First Place, and the only way I knew back then to make this happen was to keep the whole thing out of my mind, which Nathan's fortune suddenly didn't allow. "I overreacted," I said on the phone, which was true. By the time I got home I was more ashamed than anything else.

Nathan handed the phone back to Bridget, and I wished her a good time on the trip to Monterey that she and Nathan were leaving for that day. "When will you be back?"

"I don't know," she said. "When we get bored, I guess. I'll call you."

They were gone for more than a week. I spent the time practicing my typing at the computer desk with the machine turned off, looking at the ghost of my reflection in the monitor. Even shadowed and distorted through the curvature of the screen I could tell she was sad, so to cheer her up I started typing letters to James. I never turned the machine on. I didn't have an address in the desert, so I figured I didn't have a reason to actually produce anything. It was enough just to point out letters every few seconds, poking at keys as if at dead pets.

> James, i miss you, and even if i knew where to find you i couldnt get there because my car is still sitting in the driveway untouched. when i told my dad i was going to find the keys and steal the car one night he said okay but i keep them in my underwear. eww.

Going slow made it hard to keep track of what I had just said, and without a screen to tell me, I had to think hard about it. But somehow it was better than talking, like the time over Christmas break when we went to the beach and he told me he loved me. Afterward we didn't say a word to one another for more than an hour.

> i keep thinking of that day i think because where you are there is probably a lot of sand. and i remember the sand that stuck to the side of your body when you laid back and closed your eyes. and i remember the sound of the waves. ive heard that sound all my life but that day they sounded louder than ever. it was so warm for december.

I did this for days, hiding myself in a corner of the house and avoiding both my dad and Conrad, who may have died from so much neglect. I typed anything. This time it didn't matter. I typed

> what i like best about you sometimes is how light your arm feels around my shoulders.

and

> my period came today. right on time. not that we should have been worried, of course. i just know how you get grossed out.

and

when you get home we should go shopping because you are probably losing a lot of weight and your old clothes may not fit.

and

mantarayparkerjuniorbaconcheeseburgertimemachinewashmyhairofthedogs andcatsonbroadwaytogofuckyourselfhelplthelessfortunatesonofagunshotinthe heartofglasseyeintheskybluebloodbankoftheswissmissyoumissyoumissyoumiss youmiss

until my dad eventually found me. "What's all that racket?"

"Just practicing."

He was just back from work and had a drink in his hand. "I can't figure it out," he said. "Is it that you're spoiled? Or just stupid?"

He stood over me like a rickety stepladder.

"You tell me, Erica. How did I raise you? Is it because you're spoiled and lazy that I come home from work and find you sitting here clattering at a computer you haven't even turned on? Or are you just stupid? I know I've seen it on before, so hell—maybe you are. Maybe you plan to sit around all summer and wait until your mean old dad comes to his senses and gives you those keys, but I'll tell you what—it ain't gonna happen. I'm not raising a spoiled rich girl. You're taking a test by the end of the week."

"*Why are you being so mean to me?*" I was crying and couldn't look up at him.

"Hey, I'm doing you a favor, kiddo." He tossed a bunch of envelopes into my lap. They skidded off my bare knees and onto the floor. "There's your mail."

My fingers were sticky from rubbing at my eyes and a few of the envelopes got wet, but it didn't matter. Most of them were more communiqués from UCLA about registrations and dorm life. And then stuck in the middle of the pile was something handwritten, letters curled like little bugs in blue ink, which I recognized as the ugly script of my boyfriend. *Magic.*

Erica,

We stopped today in Yucca Valley and they let us send letters at the post office. The last two weeks have been pretty gnarly. I twisted my ankle on a hike and had to be carried to the next resting stop. Then Bret, our guide, helped me make a crutch out of a fallen branch, so for a couple days I was hopping around like a gimp. Some of the other kids here are FUCKED UP, like Wes who broke somebody's jaw in a fight at school and John who's only fifteen but got caught selling coke. There's even a girl here. Her name is Melissa and she trashed her boyfriend's car, so I told her we have something in common! Except that she did it on purpose after he broke up with her. She smashed it to pieces with a sledgehammer. The food sucks, though one night Bret trapped and killed a rabbit which was pretty good. I'm tired of taking a dump in a hole and everything I own smells like a campfire. And I'm supposed to never drink and drive again? Maybe I won't, but every night I sleep in a bag and count the days until we can party again. Today it's thirteen. Did you get that car yet?

Gotta go.

Love,

J.

I counted the *I*'s, *me*'s, *my*'s and *we*'s. Thirteen. I counted the *you*'s. One—though one of the *we*'s referred also to me. I tried to hold these numbers right up next to one another as a function of how much he was missing me, but all they could tell me was that James was focusing on himself and his experiences right now, and James always focused on himself and his experiences, and I never minded, because after a year of dating him I considered myself such a large part of both. All he and I did in those days was date one another, and because I was going to college in LA and he would be getting a job in LA, I imagined that we'd continue to date one another until some terrible accident happened, such as severe disfigurement or my falling in love with one of my professors. Until that time, it wasn't that I lived for him exactly, but when I read in his letter that he was looking forward to riding around in my still unnamed car it was enough to say, Screw you, Dad, and do the work I had to do to get those keys in my hand by the time he got home. But I couldn't start right that moment or else my dad would've thought he won, so I took James's letter up to my room and spent the rest of the night there, painting my nails with magic markers and responding to none of my dad's apologies through the door.

I left my room the next morning, after Dad had gone to work, and ate peanut-butter toast for breakfast. Also, I brewed a pot of coffee. Conrad was his usual self when I pushed in the appropriate disks and booted his program up, all *S*'s and enthusiasms, making me feel good about the decision I'd made to practice each finger separately. I started with the right pinky, resting on that semicolon, because I'd need even useless fingers if I wanted to beat my dad. And I wanted to beat my dad more than anything. I stuck a motivating image in my head of Dad cradling the keys before me as if handing over his last shred of dignity. It seemed to work. Before today my motivation had been James and the image of us blazing down the highway with the top down, speeding toward places more challenging and strange than the ones we'd spent our lives acclimating to. It had always been clear that he and I had a kind of dependency on cars, so learning to type before he got back to town was more than just preparing myself for some distant career. It was to save the thing that brought us together, and that morning, locked as I was on the image of Dad groveling, I realized that

I now had to do the hard work that Dad couldn't do—or wouldn't do—to keep Mom around.

It didn't take me long to learn what everyone already knew: typing is just memory, it's just burying certain repetitive movements so deep in your bones that typing desire becomes like a laser beam from brain to fingertips. After two hours my eyes were bleary and itchy from staring at the screen, but I got to the point where if I saw Conrad slither under an *a* or a *z*, my left pinky would kick up automatically, as if the world's tiniest doctor had tapped it with a mallet. Later, I was lying on the couch when the phone rang, and I was glad to hear it was Bridget, asking me what was up as if she hadn't been gone for days.

"I drank too much coffee," I said. "But you're back! How was your trip? Did you come up with a name for the car?"

"Oh, I didn't even think about it."

I found this irresponsible. "Well, what did you do all week?"

There was a pause before she spoke, and I knew in that pause she was taking an important breath. *Oh, no.*

"We had sex," she said.

"Oh my god, come over."

I sat up and rubbed my eyes and felt very aware of my body. My feet were slopped against the floor and my brain was floating in fluids. I didn't feel ready to properly deal with Bridget's news, so before she arrived I drank a tall glass of milk and stood under a shower so hot it scalded me pink and made my scalp a different kind of tingly. She rang the doorbell and I answered it in my robe, my hair wrapped girlishly in a towel.

"So how was it?"

She followed me into the kitchen and grabbed a Diet Rite from the fridge. "It was so amazing," she said. "I've never felt closer to him. It's like this whole cosmic thing. It's like you're joined together."

"Well, you *are.*"

"I know but it's more than that. It's just—I wish I'd done it earlier, you know? It's just so incredible. It's like the greatest feeling."

I felt I was supposed to be asking more specific questions about what he did and where he touched and kissed her and what he said and whether it hurt, but I didn't have the interest. Maybe I was a prude, but I had done enough of the other stuff to James to prove myself otherwise, and there was something about how fully Bridget was gushing about the experience that made me a little distrustful.

"You should sleep with James when he gets back," Bridget said. "Then we'll both know."

It was an idea.

Out in the living room the clock on the mantel chimed noon and I stood and waited out its twelve slow dingdongs. Bridget checked some of her cuticles. She asked when James was getting back and I said four days and told her about the letter he sent and the test my dad wanted me to take. "I still need to practice some more," I said.

"God, really? Didn't you practice while I was gone?"

I told her I wasn't much in the mood when all the people in my life were gone and out breathing salt air and letting their skin get brown naturally. "So James is miserable shitting in a hole," I said. "At least he's outside." My own cuticles were pristine and boring. "This summer sucks."

"I can't take this," Bridget said, killing her soda. "I can't take your moping. Just take the test, Erica. Just win or pass or whatever. Then we'll have the car and we can get you out of the house."

So it was *we* now.

As she left I called out behind her. "If I get the car and you still don't have a name, no way am I letting you inside."

Maybe it wasn't true, but if a fire was being lit under my ass I wasn't going to be the only one burned.

Every day for the next three days I took practice tests after breakfast and after dinner. I didn't run any drills. I didn't clack empty messages into an unbooted machine. I just took the tests as if my dad were standing over my shoulder and did my best to keep my eye on Conrad and throw my fingers wherever he demanded. By the end of the third day my wpm score was forty-nine. I looked at the number printed in big block text, Conrad bouncing in place with his tongue wiggling proudly, and thought: *Eleven.* Eleven more words per minute. "Eleven more words per minute" was only five words, which wasn't even half of eleven. Before going to bed that night I typed *eleven more words per minute* sixty times in the hopes that numerology might visit me over the night and save the day.

But nothing visited. In the morning I saw my dad in the kitchen and he said, "Test today," and I said, "Let's just do it right now."

I made him wait in the other room. I told him to shut the door and not to make a single sound. "How do I know you're not cheating?"

"Dad, if I could figure out a way to cheat on this program I'm sure I'd be able to ride the wave of the future without superior typing skills."

"Touché," he said and sat himself at the far end of the couch.

And then I just slogged through. By that point I wasn't able to type without watching my fingers, so I kept my face far from the monitor, shifting my gaze up and down rather than bending my head. I thought I could save time that way. Conrad served me some gems. *Heather's departure came quickly, and her return arrival was late.* And: *Their mother went shopping for bandages, cookies, and pink leg-warmers.* And: *Yesterday's science quiz included a few multiple choice questions; no true-false.* I tripped up a lot on the punctuation because I spent brainpower trying to figure out whether it was grammatically correct or just there to complicate the test. Did Conrad truly understand the semicolon? Did I, for that matter? It looked to me at last like a snake, sneaking itself into the rough of sentences and leaping out to bite my absentminded pinky. The sentences came quickly. I kept moving my fingers where they were supposed to go. Slowly I began to feel like a machine, geared and chugging, a robot built for efficiency, and before I could react to this feeling the last sentence was all typed out and the test was over. The whole thing took maybe four minutes.

When Conrad needed to calculate my score, he'd pop up largely on the screen, foreshortened toward the tail, and deliver a typing tip, some nugget of advice like an electronic cookie fortune. This time around, I got a strange one. *Most typists have a dominant hand that gets more use than the other. It's okay if this hand strays outside its boundaries every now and again. Just don't get your fingers twisted up!* Was this even true? Before I could get an answer, I got my score: fifty-five.

"Five more words per minute" was also five words, and also much faster to type.

I thought about what to do. Did Dad know how long these things took? Was there time for a take two? "How's it going in there?" he called, and then he knocked on the door, which then opened. "Done?"

"Yeah."

The fifty-five was large enough on the screen for him to see it. We both stared at it for a while. "I'll take another one tomorrow," I said.

"Forget about it," he said.

The keys went *thud* on the desk and sat there like a spitball; I almost couldn't touch them.

"Isn't this how spoiled rich girls get what they want?" I said, looking down at the keys because I didn't want to turn around and see what my dad's face might be doing. "I wonder if Mom would have given in so easily."

"Your mom's gone, Erica," he said.

As if I didn't know.

"Whatever," I said, poking at certain computer keys just to put some noise in the room. "I don't feel very adult right now."

"Me neither," I heard him say. "Best get used to it."

I went out to the car and tried to drive somewhere but couldn't think of anywhere to go. Plus I felt bad driving her around namelessly, so I just sat inside with the top down and set my radio stations and put the seat in recline and took a little nap in the sun. In my dozing I saw Alan sitting at Bridget's dining table. A bottle hanging from his face. His slouched and arrogant posture. His hair cropped close and parted like Hitler's. If it was a dream he said *hey* in the dream. Then he said he told me so.

At four I called James's house to see if he was home and he was. "You didn't call me immediately?" I said.

"I just got home like fifteen minutes ago."

"Come over and see my new car."

"Now?" he said. "Why can't you drive over here later?"

"I'm not dealing with your mom," I said. "Come over."

After dinner his folks' BMW pulled up behind my Alfa Romeo. I watched from the porch and ran to meet him in the driveway, where he stood in his surfer shorts and Stüssy shirt, looking rougher and more compact than before, as if he were keeping more of himself from me. "You're so dark," I said. It looked like he'd been whittled out of some hobo's walking stick. "And so tiny."

He stuck his keys in his pocket and kept his fist in there, defiant. "I'm not tiny."

"You are," I said, grabbing at him like a prize. "That's why I love you." I nosed in past his ear and smelled his hair, which smelled mostly of boy sweat, but that boy was James so I was happy to breathe it in for a while. Then I pulled back to kiss him, but when I did I noticed something new. Something red like warning signs and purple like the stupid tights of a court jester. It stared out at me from his neck like an angry eye.

"What's that?" I asked.

"What?" he said.

First he tried to call it a bruise and then he tried to call it a shaving burn. As if he shaved. But we both knew what it was and we knew it was called a hickie because we'd spoken so often about how stupid they were on the people who would brandish them like medals around the hallways of our school. We'd hold hands while we passed them and agree that hickies were for careless, childish people. We'd agreed never to inflict one on each other.

Or at least I'd agreed.

"Things got out of hand one night," he said. "I don't have her number. I'm not going to call her."

Melissa. The girl who smashed up her boyfriend's car was named Melissa. I thought about whether or not to let myself cry.

"We didn't even do anything," he said.

"You did this," I said and pressed it like a button.

I told him to go home and not to call me.

"Don't you want to show me the car?" he said.

"*Don't touch it,*" I said. "Just go home and look her up in the phone book and you can make out like teenagers the rest of your life."

I'd made it to the screen door and opened it when he said, "But we *are* teenagers." I tried to slam it shut, but with its auto-cush-ioned hinge I could only throw it forward a few feet on its lazy arc.

* * *

The next day Bridget and I were sitting in the Romeo. The top was down and overhead the sun was vengeful, and I was worried our sweat would ruin the leather seats. "Should we put the top up?"

"No way," Bridget said. She fooled with the radio and tried to find something peppy. "So it's over between you two?"

James had called twice that morning and I told my dad to say I was here, sitting in the same room but completely unaware that the phone was even ringing. He hated James, of course—the thug who drank himself into a car accident with his daughter sitting shotgun, totaling her car and forcing him to buy her another—so he was all too happy to comply.

"Where do you want to go?" I asked.

"Oh," she said. "Wherever. Don't you want your name first?"

"What name?"

"For the car: it's Pamela."

Pamela had curves and it had attitude. Subdued and fierce. It was my mother's name.

"I don't know why I didn't think of it before."

"That's smart, Bridge. *Pamela,* not Pam. Never Pam, okay?"

"Okay."

It was time for a drive. I turned the key and revved Pamela up a little until I felt goofy and stopped. We pulled out of the driveway carefully and turned her down all the roads that led away from my house. We were seventeen. We were seventeen in the summertime and had the whole world in front of us. "Let's go to the canyon." Bridget just leaned back in her seat and closed her eyes and bathed in the sun. I sped Pamela up the on-ramp to the 405 and the engine's growl made me smile like a drunk, and I got her all the way to seventy-five before all the cars became a wall and I had to stop and fit myself in like a puzzle piece and wait. We sat there and felt the sun on us. Five minutes later we hadn't budged.

Karl Friedrich Gauss

WE WERE TOLD TO SPEND THE REST OF THE PERIOD figuring out a ten-letter word we could type using only the top row of keys for extra credit, but I already knew it from my *Mensa Book of Trivia*, so I wrote it down on a small piece of paper with my hand curled around so Danny wouldn't try to cheat. I turned it in and spent the rest of the period not even touching my keyboard but instead telling Danny that I was smarter than he was and how I was like Gauss when he was asked to add the numbers 1 through 100 inclusive and he did it in two minutes.

Do you know how he did it, Danny? I asked Danny. Do you? I do. It's easy. Do you want me to tell you?

And Danny said, Shut up. I'm trying to come up with a word.

I didn't tell Danny, because then he would know something I knew and he'd be a little less dumber than I am. I put emphasis on the word "little" because there's so much more that I know than Danny knows. Except sports. But all sports is is memorizing facts and statistics and sports hardly ever comes up on *Jeopardy!* In

Trivial Pursuit, I usually save green for the end and then wait until the question is Leisure, because those are often about food which I know everything about. For example, the tomato is technically a fruit but legally a vegetable because of a Supreme Court decision made back before I was born. So if you called a tomato a fruit in the produce department it could sue you for damages.

I was bored because I'm usually bored in my elective classes, so I decided to play one of the creativity games I've invented. I've invented eight creativity games so far and I hadn't yet tried out my latest one because I'd just invented it the day before, so I turned back to Danny and asked him, Hey Danny, what's the opposite of a gun? He kept staring at his keyboard as if he could ever figure out the ten-letter word as fast as I could so I said it again. Danny, what's the opposite of a *gun*?

And he said, Shut *up*, Morris. You're so stupid. A gun is an object and objects don't have opposites.

I laughed really loud so everyone could know how funny I thought Danny was and I said, A black pawn in chess is an object and clearly its opposite is a white pawn. And anyway, it's a creativity game that I invented so you're not supposed to be so literal. Just say something, okay?

Ms. Jericho said, Owen. Shh.

And Danny said, Play your own game. He said it under his breath but Ms. Jericho heard him and shh'd again.

So I said, If you play I'll give you the answer to the keyboarding puzzle.

And Danny said, Okay what was the question?

I repeated the question of the *What's The Opposite Of A Gun?* creativity game and watched Danny look up at the ceiling and think of an answer. He always looks up at the ceiling to think of answers. When I finish tests all those minutes before the rest of the class I sometimes watch Danny look up at the ceiling, and one of these days I'm going to play a trick on him and put a message on a piece of paper and stick it on the ceiling so that when he gets stuck on a test and looks up there to think of an answer, he'll read my message, which will say something clever like, Check the floor stupid, or, Owen is fabulous.

Danny opened his eyes after forever and said, Okay I got it. The opposite of a gun is a hospital, because guns can kill and hospitals can heal. And I clapped once and said, Aha! and before Ms. Jericho could shh me I told him what his answer meant for him as a personality archetype. I said, See, Danny, that's very interesting because all you can think of when I say "gun" is a thing that kills people, but guns aren't this by definition, are they? When you look up "gun" in the dictionary does it say right there, you know, noun, number one, thing that kills people? I could tell Danny would take a long time thinking this through so I did it for him and said, No, it doesn't. A gun *can* kill people, but it doesn't have to kill people. So do you think "hospital" is the real opposite of a gun?

Most of the kids were packing up their bags because we had only three minutes left until the end of the period, and like she always does Ms. Jericho was shouting not to pack up because we could do a lot of work in three minutes. Danny noticed this like I did and said, Come on, I played your stupid game now tell me the answer. He had his pen in his hand, the fat kind with black and blue and red and green inktubes inside. He clicked the green which was his favorite and held it over the paper, thinking I was just about to tell him the answer. But I wasn't going to tell him the answer because to play *What's The Opposite Of A Gun?* you have to go back and forth. Like all of my creativity games, *What's The Opposite Of A Gun?* is an exchange of ideas so that both sides get something out of playing. I wasn't going to learn anything from his answer, so I intended to have him learn something from mine, which I knew was the only right answer to give.

I said, No I'm not going to tell you the answer because you haven't asked me what I thought the opposite of a gun was. Aren't you going to ask me?

And Danny said, Fine.

And I said, Fine, what?

And he said, Fine, I'm asking you.

And I said, Asking me what?

And he punched me in the shoulder like he always does and actually said, Fuck, but Ms. Jericho was still carrying on about not packing up and she didn't hear him. He said, Fuck, Morris, what the fuck is the opposite of a fucking gun already?

And I said, You don't have to get obscene. But I'll tell you what I think. I think the opposite of a gun is a flower and here's my rationale. A gun is man-made, and it's made of metal, and it's usually black or metallic grey in color. Also a gun is symbolic for destruction, which as you can clearly see is not the same as saying it kills people. And a flower is none of these things. Flowers are made by nature and they are very colorful and they are symbolic for growth and profluency. So if you ask me, I'm telling you: the opposite of a gun is a flower.

Danny said, That sounds like something a sissy would say, except he didn't say "sissy," he said the F-word that my dads told me never to say so I won't repeat it here. I told him that he shouldn't say that word but he just rolled his eyes at me, which like punching me in the shoulder he does a lot, and asked me once again for the answer. Quick, Morris, he said. The bell's about to ring.

But then the bell did ring and Ms. Jericho called out to the class, Class, okay, time is up on the extra-credit brainteaser. And most people moaned and picked up their backpacks and put them on their backs but only with one strap because two straps was what most people thought was uncool. Danny punched me again in the shoulder, right where he did before and where a subsequent bruise had begun to form, so that it hurt by my estimates triply so, and he said, Thanks a lot, sissy, but I trust I don't have to tell you what he really said. And then Ms. Jericho said that only one person had come up with the answer, and when she asked me to inform the rest of my classmates I was in a kind of funny mood after having successfully played *What's The Opposite Of A Gun?* for the first time so I stood up on my chair and I said, The word, classmates, is "typewriter." And then I took a bow and when I came back up a spitball hit me in the lower right eyelid, which caused my eye reflexively to shut as a form of protection, and this, combined with the speed at which I brought my hand to my face to wipe away the spitball, threw me a little off balance on my chair and I fell in a crash to the floor. My keyboarding classroom wasn't carpeted like my math classroom was, so when my elbow and coccyx hit the ground they had only the dirty linoleum to cushion the blow, which of course wasn't much. The other students laughed from somewhere outside my field of vision, and when I turned my head to get my bearings I saw a few who had started to leave the room come back in and look at me there on the floor. They pointed with their index fingers and did other things with their middle ones and Danny said, Serves you right, and kicked me in the ribs. I decided that it would behoove me to lie there until everyone had left, and when Ms. Jericho stepped up next to me and held out her hand I took it as a sign that the coast was clear, at least for now.

I left keyboarding and went through the halls and went through my day, which was like every day before it and which will probably be like the 484 school days laid out before me before I can graduate and leave town for a university. I am not Karl Friedrich Gauss even though I felt like him after getting the extra credit right away. I would probably not become aware in time of the fact that all the numbers 1 through 100 include fifty pairs of sums totaling 101, adding up then to 5,050 when all has been said and done. I only know this now because I read it in a book. But my dads tell me that thinking is a job and people can only do a good job if they work really hard at it and I think always. I think about what a bruise is made of and I think about how the word for a bundle of sticks transformed into something pejorative and I think about where to walk and how to step through the halls so that I don't draw attention, because on the way from keyboarding to gym I have to walk down the senior hallway in order to make it on time, and while none of them probably even know who Gauss is they are larger than I am, large like aircraft carriers, and some of them carry in their one-strapped backpacks not the opposite of a gun, but the opposite of the opposite of a gun, and if the seniors are aircraft carriers and if I show up on their radars as even a small blip, I will feel whatever it is they have in their arsenal and I will feel it immediately and I'll feel it past bedtime.

Smear the Queer

AS A KID I HAD A PERPETUAL COWLICK AND A MEAGER collection of autographs I kept in an envelope at the back of my underwear drawer. The cowlick I tackled with hand-me-down ballcaps and the autograph collection I sorted alphabetically by last name. It was a short-lived collection. One of the last autographs I asked for was that of Vince Lombardi, who made at the other end of our county a one-time appearance I begged my mother for weeks to take me to, and by the time we arrived the line of fans waiting to meet the man who had rekindled the energy and spirit of Washington's football franchise, to say nothing of the things he did for Green Bay, stretched all the way back to the entrance of Hecht's. This was in 1972. Lombardi had retired three years previously. I stood in line for twenty minutes before it became clear that I had to use the bathroom, and though it would have been simple for my mother to hold my spot while I darted out of line, she'd left to get some shopping done. At the thirty-minute mark it was impossible to stand still. I jigged and I toe-tapped. Directly behind me stood a hefty man in loose shorts holding an 8 × 10 glossy of the coach in his two broad hands. These I saw at eye level every time I'd swivel around to find my mother, and behind them at certain angles I could see the swell of his belly stretch his T-shirt's cotton. I looked up once at his moustache and found an open mouth grinning down at me, and in my shame I turned away and that's when I lost all control. I remember the waxy green plants clustered in wood-veneer boxes at the center of the mall's main corridor, large leaves jutting everywhere like the oars to some sinking lifeboat. With every step I took toward the coach's table I felt one thigh pull at the skin of the other through the tight bond of wet denim. My mother returned just before I reached the front of the line, and immediately she took my hand and marched us over to the J.C. Penney, where she bought the first pair of sweatpants she saw and shoved me toward the fitting rooms. "I don't understand why a *ten-year-old . . .*," she said. The sweatpants were crayon blue and came down to just above my ankles. I was ten years old and my ten-year-old body had failed me. I threw the soiled jeans away as soon as I got home.

For what it's worth, it wasn't until my second year at Pitt that I ever kissed anybody. He was the teaching assistant in an introductory chemistry seminar I had to take, and throughout the semester in recitation sessions I didn't say a word and Richard and I (his name was Richard Chester Van Horn) never had any reason to interact. I'd always done the reading for that week, and I cleared up during the seminar anything that may have been confusing about the difference between top and bottom quarks, say, or the eccentricities of the ion. As such, I got exceedingly good grades, to the point where I must have stood out enough to Richard that when he and I ran into each other at adjoining urinal troughs at a Panthers game the following year he remembered my name. "Richard Van

Horn," he said, reminding me of his. I ducked my head. "Last year? Chem one hundred?"

He spoke loud enough for everyone in the men's room to hear, but was polite enough not to offer his hand.

I said hello, furiously willing him away. By the time I was able to finish up and maneuver around the squarely held shoulders of three dozen game-day fans to the men's room's exit, I'd thought I'd lost him. But there he stood, waiting for me, offering his hand at last. It wasn't his attentions I was afraid of, nor, when I think about it, was it what I thought he might be after. Of myself at the time I knew only that I didn't have in me what my roommate and the other men on the floor of my dormitory did: this tug in their groins toward the women around our campus who outnumbered men 59 to 41 percent, this need in our nightly common-room confabs to bring the discussion around to women and their bodies and the things they might be doing with one another up on their floors, which were stacked in our building on top of the men's floors as if to emphasize woman's general inaccessibility to man. What I'd come to realize about the men on my floor is that they wanted to share in the bounty of women through speculation and braggadocio, as though an available woman could be manifested right on the floor of the common room if the will of the collective were great enough. My will wasn't great, is what I knew. I also knew that I couldn't look away when they showered within eyesight, no matter what my staring might have cost me. Richard must have been able to detect all this, somehow, and I remember being afraid of the conversation that would ensue. I'd only in my life to that point spoken with men who weren't available to me and women I'd wanted nothing from.

"Are you here alone?" he began things by asking.

"No," I said. "No. I'm here with my roommate."

My roommate was a generous guy named Brad who redshirted on the wrestling team and spent much of the school day seeking out parties happening over the weekend, to which he always brought me along, introducing me to women with whom he thought I would do well. If I was a disappointment, he didn't harp on it. Brad had a collection of cardboard bar coasters he kept in a high stack on his dresser, and one of women's phone numbers he wrote right on the cinder-block wall as if he were a prisoner counting the days of his sentence.

"In the student section?" Richard asked. And when I said yes he insisted I join him and "some friends" in their seats, which were closer to the 50-yard line and only twenty rows up. "Cal couldn't make it, so there's a spot and everything."

He pointed, and I followed the line of his hand to an area closer to the action, so to speak, than I'd ever been before, where the fans were older and paid better attention, and that afternoon I abandoned Brad and went with Richard Chester Van Horn. I don't remember the score of the game, but I remember that we won and that afterward I went with Richard and his friends to a bar, one in a neighborhood not adjacent to campus, one that didn't have any TVs blinking in the corners of the ceiling. I was served beers without incident and Richard made me laugh by telling me stories about hunting with his father and uncles as a kid. "I had a Ralph Lauren jacket that I always wore with matching hat and gloves," he said. "They called me 'The Gentleman Hunter.'" We sat there for hours. The night ended at one of his friends' houses, and Richard led me upstairs to a dark bedroom. The drinks gave us things to talk about, mostly our own personal histories, his much fuller than my own. It was hard, lying under his gaze, wanting my body to line up with all these bad ideas I'd developed for it. Out of modesty I let him ask most of the questions.

When one grows up as I did with three older brothers, one becomes whether one means to or not a football player. I was the requisite second man of the two two-man teams with which we turned our backyard into a ballfield, and because I was the smallest and least aggressive I was traded among my brothers like a heavy sack they had to carry. "Okay, you guys take Jim for a while," I'd hear every twenty minutes. Once none of us was happy, these football games devolved to unstructured scrumps of Smear the Queer, and my bald inability to match them on the field led me to best them off the field. I read biographies of players and histories of teams. I scoured like an occultist through the numerology of players' statistics and spent weekend mornings cleaning my room with sports-talk radio playing in the background. I held imaginary conversations with my parents' friends in which I spent upward of an hour asking them how incredible they considered the career of Don Shula. *In just two years he led the Miami Dolphins of all teams to a perfect season. When do you think we'll see the likes of that again? Huh?*

When it came time to start looking at universities I'll admit that much of my decision was based on the quality of that school's football team, and through inexplicable prejudices and allegiances I'd cultivated against the Big 8 and the SEC—two conferences I considered to be full of showboats and martyrs—I ended up at the University of Pittsburgh almost by default, unfortunately right after Johnny Majors had left, but Jackie Sherrill was crafty enough to get the ball moved swiftly down the field, and by the time I graduated with a degree in chemical engineering I was able to see the Panthers in four bowl games, and even watch them win, something not one of my brothers, all of them high school diploma-holders, had ever accomplished.

I got my first job out of college at DuPont, working in one of the company's offices outside Philadelphia on a long-term project to find safer alternatives for the chlorofluorocarbons that had recently been connected to the ozone layer's slow depletion. It was my job to explore the whole group of alkyl halides, and so I'd spend most of the workday sitting at my desk on the second floor of a three-story building, sketching chemical structure diagrams. For an hour I would erase and redraw fluoride and hydrogen ions, doubling or rebonding them, shuffling them around the way I would a strong safety in some defensive playbook. And though I knew that the end result of the job I had to do—my bread and butter, so to speak—was a saved face for a company that had been caught doing much public damage, the everyday work of it was extremely pleasurable. I had a few co-workers with whom I shared lunch hours. I had a boss who left me alone. I drove a Volvo and owned a condominium in the city.

Richard and I were never really a couple, but he'd known the right things to say that made me less awkward with later men. All the same, it had always, whether or not I like to admit it, been difficult for me to meet other men who might share, well, my interests. In Philadelphia I knew where the men who wanted to congregate with men could do so without high concern, but I never felt comfortable in those sorts of places. They were nightclubs, mostly, and any quick peep through their front doors would reveal an array of jackboots and biceps I may have wanted the pleasure of getting a closer look at were it not for all the rapidly spinning lights. Here were a hundred happy men moving as one, whereas I, for example, never went to prom. On the afternoon I met Charlie I'd been awake for thirty-three hours, having stayed up the previous night to page through the Pitt Stop catalog and circle all the items I could tell were new. Which accounts for the first two hours. I don't remember how the other thirty-one were passed, though I do know that I never missed a day of work in the seven years of my employment at DuPont. They gave me an award when I left, a walnut plaque I still have in a drawer somewhere, that reads, DEDICATION—IT STARTS WITH SHOWING UP FOR WORK, IT CONTINUES WITH DILIGENCE AND CAREFUL ATTENTION, IT ENDS NEVER. At any rate I was poorly rested that afternoon and when I came upon Charlie on the bus I thought he was my brother Bill, older than I am by eleven and a half years, because he had Bill's same crisp brush cut and Bill's same shaggy eyebrows. Bill, of course, was still living back in Virginia at the time, so imagine my surprise. I sat down right next to the man and said, "Bill! Hi!" Every head on the bus turned to mine and I asked Bill what he was doing here.

"My name is Charlie," he said.

I looked down at his hands and saw he was twiddling a guitar pick down the ridges of four thin fingers, and that's when I realized my mistake. Bill has always had the hands of a drunken mafioso. So I apologized and explained the situation of my being sleep-deprived, and Charlie seemed such a good sport about the blunder that I offered to buy him a drink someplace nearby. "Shall we get off at the next stop?" I asked. I was sure to hold his eyes with my own. After years of living in a city as large as Philadelphia I'd become adept enough at understanding how much from a man could be read in the eye that I was able to sort all men into three groups. This worked particularly well with strangers seen across restaurants or queued up in civic offices. Men whose eyes met yours and then looked immediately elsewhere, as though they were taking a brief survey of the people in the room who might try to do them harm, comprised the Group of Surefire Peril. I paid this group little attention. Men whose eyes met yours and stayed put long enough to effect in you a heartbeat like a fire alarm comprised the second group. This was the Group of Feasibility. But the third group, men whose eyes met yours and lingered one, two seconds before falling to the floor, then finding their way back up again, meeting yours, lingering, falling, and then lingering and falling, doing this little dance of glimpses and peeks—these men formed the Group of Unsound Conclusions, and back in those days it was these men I found myself almost daily trailing after.

Charlie's eyes met mine and fell and met mine again. He was a self-styled singer-songwriter who moved to a different city every couple years or so. "I get restless," he said. By design he moved alternately to cities where he knew a lot of people and cities where he knew few if any. He'd been in Philadelphia three months. "I don't know anybody yet," he said. "Not really." Though he looked as old as Bill he was a year younger than I was, and he was a vegetarian. When he wasn't alone in his room recording his songs—which he described as "minimalist folk with no vocal emoting"—and making copies of his demo tape, he was out on the street trolling through bars and asking whether he could audition for a gig. I thought about getting his autograph. All this I learned over the next several hours, at the sandwich shop where Charlie ate a hummus wrap and I did the same for the sake of camaraderie, at the sports bar that was only a couple blocks from my condominium where he drank gins and tonic and I drank beer and tried to avoid the TVs all around us broadcasting the Eagles' gleeful triumph over the Redskins, at the danceclub where it was so hard to talk to one another that we soon ended the evening back at my place. I'd known him for nine hours, but he had a trunk as broad as a contrabass and a backside like twin bowling balls. It was only after I had him lying facedown on my bed that he told me he'd never done anything like this before, and at first I didn't believe him. Then he looked so shyly over his shoulder at me I found myself made stupid, ready to believe anything.

At the end of the eighties I stopped traveling westward through the state for homecoming games, after Pitt hired from nowhere coach Paul Hackett, a man unable to produce a winning season, and thus began the gloomy and pessimistic years of my fandom. When the Pitt Stop catalog would come in the mail I still read it through from one cover to another, but I no longer held a pen in my hand while doing so. New recruits were names I'd never heard of and soon forgot after their freshman seasons. The Panthers were a team so lackluster that no networks bothered to send camera crews out to the stadium, and so my TV was kept tuned elsewhere, and Charlie was long gone, off to Austin where he knew everybody. It took a while to meet anyone else, but given all the kicks in the teeth going on in the NCAA it seemed in those days imperative that I do so. And how did I do it? One could scour over the highly coded pages in back of the alternative newsweekly and find sometimes a date by the weekend, though I was never very good at dating. Instead, I fell back on my preferred methods. Whether or not I had any control over it, those were the days I straggled among the Group of Surefire Peril, and while it may reveal something unseemly about my character I feel I should confess I can't remember any of their names. I remember instead all their sad overtures. Once, a man dropped his drawers just inside my entryway but kept his coat on the whole time. Once, a handgun holstered to a hairless leg. Once, even, a co-worker. I remember taking great care. I remember always taking great care, and toilet stalls with misspelled graffiti—*Leave day and time I will be here weakly.* Most of all I remember being left to fall asleep alone, always alongside a new vacancy, the bedclothes soiled and clung to my stomach.

If it was a weekend, I was out wandering, but during the work-week my days grew longer and longer as the country stood idly by awaiting Operation Desert Shield, and I was moved with the increase in demand over to Kevlar. There I worked on a team charged with making the fabric lighter yet stronger and therefore more expensive, and one late night in my cunning I was able to nab two state-of-the-art helmets. They were brown and beige and sandy and in my hands felt as light as two dried gourds. On a whim that Christmas I gave them to my parents. They'd come up that year to Philadelphia with my brothers, and on Christmas morning I made them open the boxes together. We all sat around my living room to watch, and when they realized that the helmets were helmets their faces changed. Each of their eyebrows inverted. "A helmet!" my father said, and my mother said, "A helmet?"

"It's what I'm working on now," I said. "At work."

My father tried his on and made as though he were carrying a rifle. We all laughed except our mother, who frowned and placed hers back in the box. "I guess all's I need now's a motorcycle," she said. I told her it was a war helmet and that seemed to get her more upset. To break the tension, Kevin started handing out his gifts. We were cramped in that condo, my folks in the spare bedroom upstairs and Kevin down on the couch, Bill and Dan in hotels with their wives. It had been my idea to haul everyone up from Virginia and why? What we had in Philadelphia to celebrate the holidays was what every city in the world had. A public outdoor ice rink. Malls with Santas. Downtown's unspectacular tree. Bill's birthday fell on the 26th—a Saturday, if I remember—and rather than celebrate one last night together with cake, everyone decided to beat the traffic on I-95. Cleaning out the guest room, I found the helmets in the closet with a note written in my father's hand: *Save these for the troops, son, but we sure do appreciate the thought!*

And then I heard from Charlie. He called one night after I was already in bed but before I'd been able to fall asleep. It had been three years since we last spoke, and knowing his restlessness I wondered where he was calling from, where he may have been living these days. He spoke to me very, very softly. I suddenly had so little to say. It was a warm night. I watched the fan in the corner swivel its head from one side of the room to the other. Then he apologized and said, "I shouldn't have lied to you," and I hung up the phone and let myself breathe in and out a few times. I smoothed the bedsheets and cleared some dust from my endtable, where a tall glass of water caught the light and threw it around the room at new angles. The water inside was lukewarm. Room temperature. I saw my body as a loose group of cells strung together. Transmission, I knew, was an act of will, not an act of fate or luck. *You should have been smarter,* I told myself. *You are a scientist and you should have been smarter.*

The Kevlar project was short-lived. Administrations changed and thus did intracorporate priorities and I started to get shuffled around a lot. I was moved to a position in the research and development department working with organic polymers, and then I went over to Corian. All this happened very rapidly, and it was around that time that the hairs on my crown had left in such dramatic numbers that I started to shave my head close, like a grunt. It made me look more mature, I thought, but the real bonus was that my cowlick at last was tamed. It was a minor victory, but this was a time for minor victories. One day I was called in to human resources and asked to tender my resignation. They could no longer find suitable employment for me, the lady said. Many internal changes to the company were being undertaken, she said, and the cost of retaining me as an employee was greater than the benefits my work provided the company. She was sorry that she had to let me go, she said, as if this were her decision—and maybe it was, made one morning over coffee by a complete stranger, this married woman whose name I had seen on internal company documents but with whom I'd never spoken face-to-face. We had this conversation in her office two or three weeks after I began antiretroviral therapy, and seropositivity was not just a new vocabulary word but also my new status, forcing me to track T cell counts like I once tracked rushing yards and QB ratings. I couldn't help notice during our interview this human resources executive keeping her distance from her side of the desk. They offered me a respectable severance package and the people in my team threw me a going-away party with cake and punch. I got that plaque from the company and a gift certificate to Waldenbooks, one I never bothered to cash in.

Over the next few months I sold my condominium and left Philadelphia. I had plans to do as Charlie himself did and move someplace where I knew no one and where no one knew me. All my life I'd followed whatever men I felt could lead me somewhere, and yet I never found a way to fall in love with them, never felt that emotional urgency coming from somewhere noble inside me. It was a failure of the heart, one I meant in my travels to correct, but at night when I tried to picture my life in a strange new city I wasn't able to see anything past the end of my bed, so I abandoned anything so romantic and moved back to Virginia, making trips home to see the family much more cost-efficient. This was right around the time the movie *Philadelphia* came out, which my parents told me was very good—"Very sympathetic, Jim," my mother said—but the only film I remember seeing that year was *Dave,* which I went to alone, and found with its themes of disguise and benevolent hoodwinking to be a far better fantasy. One scene has Kevin Kline sitting in the Oval Office with Ving Rhames, who plays a secret service agent, and Kevin Kline is giving Ving Rhames some ideas about a softer and less intimidating wardrobe. Kevin Kline suggests maybe wearing a sweater sometime. "You don't think a sweater would make my neck look too big?" Ving Rhames asks, and the line is played deadpan for comedy, but I went home touched and caught up in appearances, wondering what new clothes I might try on, what sort of political celebrity I might ever be mistaken for.

In the fall of 1997 it seemed likely that Pitt was headed to its first bowl game in nine years, and that Thanksgiving my brothers arranged a game of touch football in our parents' backyard as some exercise in nostalgia to pass the time while the food was warming in the oven. We hadn't played together in years, and twenty or thirty minutes were spent deciding whether I could fill my historic position as fourth man or whether it would be our father. That morning I had vomited up my egg breakfast, and hours later I remained glossed in a heavy sweat, the Pitt sweatshirt I wore blotched dark in the armpits despite the thirty-one degrees on the outside thermometer. Everyone insisted I rest except our dad, who made mention of his back that had in sixty-six years grown tight and gnarled like a bulb of ginger. "Just don't overdo yourself," he said. I assured my brothers I could play and assured Bill, my teammate, we would win. He and I shook hands in agreement, and his was so cool and so dry I wanted to wear it for a while like a glove I could wipe my leaking brow with. We boys scrambled back and forth through the long backyard, running makeshift plays and cutting jerky twists around one another to avoid any outstretched hands. I remember feeling good about being outside. I remember running and trying to breathe deeply and Dad's stepping periodically out on the deck to sip from his beercan and laugh with us at every dropped pass. Bill's kids and Dan's were glued to video games in the basement but I wished they were outside with us. Historically I've never enjoyed having an audience but that afternoon I felt the need for one, just to have someone to look at whenever Bill or I scored another touchdown, someone whose enjoyment precisely matched my own despite having had no participation in the play. It was just the four of us, though, and as the turkey took longer than our mother had expected we continued to play far longer than we should have. I missed a pass at one point and when I turned back to face Bill I saw him from an alarming distance, looking small and unrecognizable, like a child's action toy tossed into a corner of the schoolyard. And then the air around me seemed to melt and whatever breaths I could take came into my chest like short needles. All of a sudden the sun was gone. I fell to the frozen ground and all my brothers started saying my name at once.

People like to talk a lot about sports on TV and on twenty-four-hour sports-talk radio, and when they do, these people talk about football as a kind of war, with coaches as generals sending men out on the battlefield and the rhetorical refiguring of offensive and defensive strategies and so on, but I've never had much truck with these metaphors. Football has never been a battle to me, but rather a celebration, some gruff Bacchanalia where men come together for its own amazing sake. This was the feeling in the backyard every afternoon my brothers shuffled me from team to team—*We are brothers, us four, and let's see what we can do together.* Even between the hoariest of archenemies, bad blood spilled all over the field, downed players are helped up off the ground, asses are patted, scoring players are bear-hugged and tossed like mortarboards in the air, all because these are things the body in its top form can accomplish, and why not show it all off? And why not come together in the tens of thousands to watch it all happen? It's important for me to remember that football is for spectators and that it cultivates fans. The goal of every war is the end of all war. Football ends with a promise of another game next weekend, another chance at physical excellence.

Soon I was lying in an ambulance with my mother on my left holding my hand and a brown-haired gentleman with some meat on his bones looking down on me and shining a penlight in each of my eyes, first one and then the other, like a game. I was breathing but I wasn't happy about it, and I wasn't sure whether the van was moving or whether it wasn't moving. "Go Pitt," the man said, shining his little light on my sweatshirt, and to this day I rank it as one of the kindest things I've ever been told. One thing I have to cede to HIV is the interminable sense it makes, the neat and clean method through which it wants to form itself over and over again inside my body, letting copy after copy stand as proof of its vitality. It comes down to chemicals going head-to-head with chemicals, and that Thanksgiving afternoon I felt the clarity of HIV's design and purpose to be something I could read and something I could appreciate, even though some mornings I wake up and can feel these chemicals carving up the vital parts of me. It's a plague, I know, and for fifteen years or more I've been living with dizzying migraines, clenched fits of bronchitis, long nights soaked in delirium and chills, and hours crouched cramped over a toilet. And yet I also know that if I were to put the virus under a microscope, if I were to be given a lab in which to do this, I would observe it for hours. I would lose sleep watching it overtake cell after cell after cell, doing its job with steady dignity.

If You Need Me I'll Be Over There

MY GRANDMOTHER LIKED TO DRINK AND CHIDE strangers, and when it came time for her to die she did it bang on New Year's Eve. This may have been for her a kind of shortfall: one lower number on the tombstone. For me, it was a hassle, her funeral cutting into a winter break I'd opted that year not to spend at home. I got the call from Jarem just minutes before leaving for a friend's party. He assured me in a clipped, loud voice that gosh, Buddy, there was no real rush. I've got home covered for now, he said and told me to enjoy my New Year's. I flew out the morning of the second, waking at five from a nervous, kicking sleep, and suffering through sleep lack the whole leg out to O'Hare, my head throbbing with the plane's increasing altitude. When I arrived in Pittsburgh, my suit jacket was wrinkled and my eyes hung dark and drooping. I looked like a zombie, and my father was the first to tell me so.

He and I drove straight to the parlor where we'd meet my brother, mother, and grandfather. It took us an hour. On the porch, my father stood by a potted plant, rocking on his heels. Wait out here a bit, he said. His pants were brightly black in the sunlight and broke at the exact right point on his shoes. I think your mom and granddad just went in, he said. I don't want to be there when they see the body.

So we gave them a few minutes and then slipped ourselves inside.

At funerals I look around at the corners of the parlor and the knees of well-wishers in an attempt to remove myself from the situation. My therapist calls this "emotional compartmentalization" and continues to give me small challenges to combat it. She told me once to call my brother sometime and say that I'm sorry I'd never told him how much he meant to me, and I bristled in my chair and looked at the corner of her office and said that he probably knew this already.

My grandmother's funeral was well attended, which made my mother happy. Even the homecoming queen showed up. I went 0 for 5 on the names of distant family members I hadn't seen since adolescence, and every yinzer aunt marveled at how far from home I'd moved. *Buddy* all the way in *Nebraska,* they lamented to one another. My given name is Christopher, but once this became too tough for toddler Jarem to utter lisplessly, he coined Buddy and it's been my name ever since. In the parlor I made a strategy: stay out of the way. My stance bore the respectful posture I copied from the blank-faced funeral directors in the back. The room we all stood around had too low a ceiling, and there was so much puce everywhere it was like we were grieving inside some digestive organ. But the real insult was the scant three flower arrangements set on faux wooden pedestals around the coffin—my mother said it hadn't been easy finding florists open on New Year's. Throughout the viewing my grandfather wouldn't leave my grandmother's side, and even as the short service began in the next room he sat weeping and gazing into the coffin. My brother pulled up a chair and made a big show of choosing to stay with him. Go be with the family, he told our mother. Jarem held a hand of my grandfather's in his own lap, petting it, and the way my grandfather kept his eyes on his dead wife the whole time lent something fetishistic to the whole undertaking.

The stock I come from doesn't believe in watching a coffin lower mechanically into the ground. We don't bear any palls, toss any handfuls of dirt on the lid. So at the cemetery, when the pastor finished saying what she was supposed to, we all just walked back to the boxy, grey limousines that had driven us up the hill to the gravesite. Here again Granddad didn't want to leave, despite the cold rain that had begun to fall. He cried and said, I love you, Momma. I'll be with you soon—as though their marriage were some happy incestuous union. Also disconcerting: his name etched next to hers on the gravestone, right there in stately small caps with a space to the right of the hyphen waiting for an answer.

I had friends who talked about getting email from their grandmothers, but given her age and my poor correspondence this was as implausible to me as unicorns and cures for cancer. We weren't close. Didn't even talk on the phone, she and I. All the same I felt I was going to miss her. I wasn't so callous to never notice the joy in her face when she'd smile at something funny. Once when I was little, Jarem publicly revealed that I'd pissed on the toilet seat, shouting it across the house on a holiday. The adults laughed in delight and my brother stood in the hall *j'accuse*-ing me with a single pointing finger, and when my grandmother said above the laughter, Do you aim where you shoot or do you shoot where you aim? I thought it was about the funniest thing I'd heard. I laughed along with all of them at no lousy expense.

After the funeral we went to a diner to eat a cheap, death-cleansing lunch: roasted chicken with boiled corn and Jell-O salad. Dessert was angel food cake, optimistically. I was the last to enter the sterile back room in which they'd corralled our hangdog bunch, and I angled for a seat by my grandparents' neighbors: the brothers who raised cattle, just a few years older than me and Jarem. I had designs on playing How Buddy's Life Would Be Different Had He Stayed And Grown Up Here, but these neighbors were already flanked by lady cousins and I was forced to sit across from teetotaling relatives who did regional theater. They asked me, Why dontcha call more often? and I played with my food and said I was so busy with classes, which came out sounding like a lie because it was one. We all kept our chitchats jovial, for my grandfather's sake. In the spirit of this, I made it a point to tell our chefwaitress her chicken was very good. This was not a lie. It would've been the best thing to happen that day, but then I finished a Friday *New York Times* crossword puzzle for the first time.

This I did in the living room of my grandparents' now half-empty house. My father sat unashamed in my grandmother's chair, and the rest of us fell around on the floor and couch and watched the evening news. Off and on, my grandfather's chin fell to his chest in a catnap, and for long stretches nobody talked. Crosswords are solved in a disorderly fashion, penning in whatever letters can be guessed at with even the smallest conviction. It's all about fitting words into their proper places, I knew, and I was amazed at how steadily these words could open up new quadrants of the puzzle to me, which in time I filled with letters that felt all kinds of wrong. But they ended up being right, so I kept at it and my father thumbed through a magazine and my brother sat near my mother and held her attention. They were talking about taking a road trip together, to visit parts of the country my sedentary father had little interest in showing her.

I always wanted to go up to New England and see the fall foliage, she said.

I know! said Jarem.

Another commercial came and I saw that IMPUDENT should have been IMPOTENT, and like that I was done with the crossword. I said, Hey, look! and they all did, including my grandfather who woke to the sound of my demands. I finished it, I said. The *Friday* puzzle. I arced the newspaper around the room like a children's librarian. I was smiling very broadly.

My grandfather squinted over at me. Behind his thick glasses his eyes looked like fault lines.

Your grandmother could never do those things, he said.

And then he was crying, again, inexplicably. Jarem got up and grabbed the box of tissues from the kitchen table. Oh, Grampa, he said, running it over to him.

Oh, Grampa.

From across the room my mother held her wide and angry eyes at me. Lemme talk to you, she said, heading to the kitchen. My father didn't move, determined to stay out of whatever was happening.

Once, my therapist asked me if I considered myself the black sheep of the family and I said no. I said, Doesn't everyone think of themselves as black sheep? Isn't it kind of vain to do so? She had this screwed-up grin on her face and asked if being vain was something I tried to avoid, but I wasn't about to answer that question. When I eventually admitted that sometimes I dreamed of being the white sheep in a family full of black ones, she asked if that was a good dream, and I said not especially.

My mother leaned one arm on a chair, trapping me in the corner of the kitchen by the aloe plants and the black-and-white television. What are you doing? she said. Would you show some respect?

I said I was sorry. I said I was just excited.

Who gets excited on the day of their grandmother's funeral? She hissed this almost, trying to keep her angry voice in a whisper.

This was a relief, considering how violently my mother could yell. I remember as a child her screaming my name when I'd sass or scratch knick-knacks and feeling it in my ears like a blunt needle.

I'm sorry, I said again.

Don't tell me you're sorry tell him you're sorry.

I looked through the doorway at my grandfather in his chair dabbing at his eyes. My brother sat on the couch and held his hand, like he did by the coffin. He wouldn't look up at me, and I wanted to hack his arms off with the axe my grandfather kept in the shed. I walked into the middle of the room and tried to come up with something to say. Had I done what my mother told me to, this would have made me sorry. A sorry member of the family. I was twenty years old and should have been able to know what to do. But I didn't. My father coughed once to break the silence, and my grandfather continued weeping.

I'll be outside, I said and grabbed my crossword off the couch.

Out on the front porch the cold wind stung my eyes and the cows from the neighbors' farm made low, hungry-belly sounds as they treaded up the hill to the barn. My grandparents' house had a wide covered porch we used to spend most of our summer visits sitting on, sweating. Now all the vinyl-strapped furniture was stored in the shed for the winter, so I sat down on the cold steps and unfolded the newspaper. The *Post-Gazette* had its own, dumber puzzle under the *Times'*, and I pulled the pen out of my pocket and got to work under the fading grey sky. Over my shoulder, the carport's large halogen lamp flickered on, and I wriggled like a squirmy boy so as not to cast a shadow on the page. It didn't work. I solved the puzzle quickly and alone. Soon, my brother would drive me back to some sad motel room we'd have to share, and after a family breakfast he'd take me back to the airport before heading in to the city, where he had a home of his own and a career of his own. Somehow he'd been able to find these things within near reach of our family.

The front door opened. It was my father with a paper plate of chicken left over from the diner. Here, he said. I know you liked this chicken.

He sat down on the step next to me. Listen, your mom lost her mother today. Cut her some slack.

Around a mouthful I said, I am.

He sat there and watched me eat. I'm used to this. Growing up, my mom worked late and Jarem had stuff like marching band and cross-country after school, so it'd often be just my dad there to make a sandwich for me. I looked back on those days fondly. I chewed and tried to taste lost tangs and crunches. Then I realized that I'd never once thanked him for the sandwiches. I'd always just asked for them.

I never seem to do the right thing, I said.

Sure you do, he said. You just need to learn the difference between what feels right and what people expect from you.

My grandfather's house was at a kind of curve in the road, and in the growing darkness, trucks rode past with their headlights on, shining at us and then bending away. My father waved at them, not out of recognition, I guessed, but as an act of courtesy.

You'll find your place, he said. Don't sweat it. He dug a hand in my shoulder to help his heavy body up. I think your brother wants to leave soon.

Tell him I'll wait in the car, I said, handing over my plate.

On our very first day together, my therapist told me that we're given families as a lesson in selfhood; first we have to define ourselves in terms of others before we know who we want to become. And when the time comes to turn into that person, she said, the difficult part is holding on to the piece of us that's part of something greater. I sat blankly in my chair and waited for her to explain, but she didn't explain, and I'd been returning week after week to try to figure it all out. I felt at odds with my family. Were they the people I took after, or people I gave something of myself to? And what something, exactly? It was as much a riddle now as Grandma's little joke had been back then. I aimed where I shot; it'd never been any kind of choice.

In the car I couldn't keep the cold off me. I shivered and sat on my hands. When the front door finally opened and my family came out on the porch to say good-bye, I got out and waved up at them. Standing solo in the driveway I made a strategy: wake early to get to breakfast on time and sit at the center of the table. In time, my brother came down to the car, and when he moved toward the door I stopped him and took the keys. I'm driving, I said, and without a word he let me.

An Uneven House

HE HAD A LOW BROW AND A HEAVY STEP, AND THAT afternoon after work was like every. From the city bus he disembarked, and then he went down the lane lined with poplars for several hundred feet until he got to the house. The walkway to the front porch was broken pieces of slate, and once again after just five steps there was his wife in the doorway. "I caught you," she said. "I heard you coming up."

"Yes," he said. "I'm noisy." He kissed her, one hand pressing her trunk to his breast. "Now head back to the kitchen."

She slipped across the floor lightly, apron strings flitting like butterfly tails. He gave her the lead. He stepped inside and felt the floor quease underneath, and he hung his brown coat on a hook behind the door, and he set his lunchpail lightly by the stairs. The air in the house smelled hot and rancid.

"Dear," she called out. "Was work okay?"

"I got stuck with another shift tomorrow night."

He saw her turn from a large pot of something simmering, and her face was wrecked with worry. She went over to him delicately. A step at a time. The ground moved in response, and he counteracted carefully toward her. In the doorway from living room to kitchen, they could embrace again, unsteadily.

"There must be other jobs," she said.

"I can't risk it," he said. He slid his hands over her body and she touched her nose to his. "We have to keep saving."

He held her face in his hands, and they kissed and soon backed away from one another. Moving apart from her was the hardest fact of his life in the house; it caused the most strain on his body. He turned on the radio, and a clarinet's clean, high lament filled the space between them. There was nothing to do in that house but wait for the day they no longer had to live there. He took stock. The collection along the front wall was growing nicely. They'd have good hunting weather, he hoped, this weekend.

"I have good news," he heard his wife say. Her aunt had called that afternoon and would be visiting after supper. Wasn't that exciting? Their first visitor?

He remembered the aunt as large and alive, not in control of herself. In this house, how would they manage it?

He said to let him know when she was no longer busy in the kitchen. "I'll go up and put my suit on."

"Oh, dear, that's not necessary," she said. "Just something clean."

It would end, he knew, in disaster.

It'd been a cloudy day when the blonde woman showed them the place, the closest house to the city he could afford, and as they stepped through its rooms he could hear its protestations at the threat of being lived in once again. The groans of floorboards and door hinges warned him not to make an offer, but he was swayed by the cost of the house relative to what he considered its value. He liked its simplicity, a thin kitchen and living room on the first floor, one tiny bathroom and bedroom on the second. There was no basement, only a tool shed out against the fence and a crawlspace under the house, where he could keep his guns and his wife the canned vegetables given to her on their wedding day by her mother. They moved in and made it a home, decorating the walls with butterfly specimens and photographs of their hometown. Within just weeks, the boards and stones of the foundation became unstuck to the ground, and one day as he'd walked from front door to the kitchen sink to wash fur and blood from his hands, he felt the house sluggishly move beneath him. The floor reared up and then sank like a seesaw, and soon it was hard for him and his wife to stay together.

He gathered rocks and construction debris from city sites, but he couldn't find any spot along the foundation to put them. She said the problem must be internal. He asked how that could be. She went inside and started wandering around while he stood outside and watched. The house didn't move, though he could hear its creakings, its murmurs. If there were someone who could fix the problem, he couldn't afford it. The only thing to do was keep the shelves and mantel bare, reposition the furniture. They remade their living habits and obtained a kind of balance. When he left the house, she'd stick to the center, where the davenport and radio and telephone all were, until he came home to fill the house's empty half.

It was in bed that they could finally be together, at the very top of the house. Here they slept closely, holding on so tightly to each other it affected their dreams.

After dinner they stood in the house's center, at opposite ends of the davenport, and planned the entrance of the aunt. He wore a sweater his wife had knit for him, his gut rumbling from the light supper she'd served. She had let her hair down. How would they show off their first house? They couldn't all stand in the doorway, could they?

"I'll try to balance it," he said. "Just stay far from the edges. Stick to the center."

"No, I should do it," she said. "I'm lighter. I can move more easily than you."

"I can move fine." He spat into the fireplace. "You'll have to show her around," he said. "She'll want to see all the furniture. That china cabinet she gave you." It had taken three thewy men to carry it inside. His fortune that they'd chosen the kitchen's front wall to line it along. The house's center. The cabinet helped steady the floor but was not unable to slide, and so they kept it empty. A case for nothing but itself.

The aunt arrived precisely at eight. He stood near the door to greet her and the wife stood against the back wall, in view, hoping to wave and draw her warmly in. The calling button made a sound like angry insects and he started a little, sharing a look of surprise with his wife. It was the first time he'd heard it.

He opened the door and welcomed the aunt. She wore what looked like five dresses over one another. "Please mind your step," he said. "Our house is a little unsteady."

And here he backed quickly to the center of the room, but not quickly enough. The aunt took one step over the threshold—one bold, sloppy step—and the house bellowed like a whale and keeled doorward with a force that kicked the wife into a kitchen chair. The aunt screamed and flailed her arms and fell right back out the door, down three wooden steps to the concrete. She began moaning. He hurried to the open doorway to apologize and saw her lying on the ground, rubbing her rump. "What spirits!" she said.

He looked over his shoulder. His wife stood anxiously in the kitchen, straining to see what had happened. He motioned for her to move to the center of the house, and as she did, he trod down to the walkway.

"Here," he said, and offered a shaky hand. "Here, can you stand?"

Lifting the aunt was a task. She leaned over the railing of the steps, breathing deeply.

"Well?" he asked. "Do you need the ambulance?"

The aunt met his eye for the first time. "I wouldn't relish waiting inside for it. Your house is cursed." She shuffled past him and looked through the open doorway at her niece's head poking up above furniture. "Honey," she called. "This house is cursed. Call me when you move."

Inside, his wife stood in quiet sobs and they prepared for an early bedtime. She went upstairs first and he stayed below and heated some warm milk with honey, which he brought to her bedside with a kiss on her forehead. He undressed and laid his sturdy body alongside hers, and she sobbed his shoulder wet.

"What will we do?" she said.

"It's all right," he said. "I'll contend with your mother if she tells her about it."

"Not that," she said, both hands rubbing her belly. "What will we do when the baby comes?"

In time, he knew, it would no longer be a part of her. It would inhabit the house and move with its own separate weight.

That weekend they boarded a bus and rode out to the last stop to spend the afternoon in a field catching butterflies. They were enthusiasts. It was how they met back at home, out stalking the field by the railroad with nets bigger than the both of them. Here in the city, he'd been surprised to find a similar spot, also by the tracks, where butterflies came by the dozen, freed from the acrid air of far-off factories.

They hunted separately, yards and yards from one another. He loved to feel the ground hold firmly under each of his thundering steps. He kept one eye on his wife and another on the stretch of land before him, turning to watch each time he saw her net arc through the air. She was so gentle with the thing, gliding through the weeds and wildflowers that brushed against her bloomers. He tore through the fields. He preferred to win his specimens ruthlessly.

A little past lunchtime, he noticed a large bird circling languidly in the air and looked over at his wife to see if she'd noticed it too. He found her yards away, face-to-face with some man, who brought something up to his face. Seconds later a whistle pierced the air, and the bird cried out in response, and he watched it dive toward his wife. He tensed and began running. The bird swooped over her head and landed on the man's arm. His wife laughed and clapped.

"Pet her," the man said, looking up at the wife. He was short and gaunt and wore an expensive gentleman's hat in green felt. "She's a friendly hawk, this one."

It sat poised on his crooked arm like a monument. At random intervals, its head would swivel around smooth and mechanically on its tufted neck. Its feathers were dark and its eyes were black.

"Here, see?" The short man held something out to her and dropped it in her hand. A red strip of flesh. "She won't hurt you. Go on."

He watched his wife try to be delicate, raising her hand slowly. The hawk moved at an instant and the flesh was plucked gone from her hand. She snatched back her hand with a gasp. "Such power," she said, and a smile opened up on her face.

"Is that a falcon?" he asked.

"Nay," the man said. "A black hawk."

"Do you hunt with it?"

"Dear," she said, "you have to feed it. Sir, do you have any more of . . . whatever you gave me?"

"Rabbit," he said, pulling another strip out of a pocket and tossed it shortly to him. It felt warm and wet and he raised the strip up above the bird like a mother's worm, lowering it close to its head. It shook and extended its wings in a mild uproar.

"Not so sudden," the short man said.

He tried again, slower this time, and when the hawk finally pecked it from his fingers he grinned. His wife smiled with him, the two of them standing side by side with butterfly nets in opposite hands, flanking them like totem poles.

The short man petted and smoothed the feathers around the hawk's head and neck. "You two catching grasshoppers?"

"Butterflies," he said.

"It's our hobby," she said.

"Any luck?"

He looked at her for a report on her findings. He'd caught a specimen that he thought was the Viceroy but turned out to be a small Monarch. She'd caught nothing of interest yet. He remembered the first specimen he'd ever given her—a Marble Warlock. He presented it from behind his back one evening at her parents' house, pinned carefully inside a case he'd made with scraps from work. On either wing was a small black circle, not half as big as a dime. On one knee, he'd said, "I'm afraid these are the only rings I can afford," and she couldn't catch her breath until her mother had sat her down.

The short man nodded down a little toward her belly. "I see you've got a little one coming. That should bring you luck."

He put one arm around his wife. "It might," he said.

The hawk started a little on the arm of the man, tugging on the short tethers that held its feet in place. The short man backed up a few paces and let the hawk go, and the couple lifted their gazes to the sky to watch it climb higher and higher. When his neck began aching he looked back at his wife. The short man was gone.

A few hours later she came scurrying across the field, one hand holding the net closed near the top. He took a look at the specimen: large and dust-colored, with downy hairs spreading over its wings and abdomen.

"What do you think it is?" she said.

It clung to the inner lining of the net, its wings ticking against the side in a nervous rhythm. "It might be the Tawny Emperor," he said.

She jumped a little, rustling the specimen. "Oh, we don't *have* one of those!"

He grabbed a glass jar out of the bag he'd brought and reached into the net, capturing the thing and tightening the lid. The sun was falling faster in the sky, and the two began making their way across the field toward the service station up the road, where the bus would come and turn around and take them back home. While they waited, he watched men drive cars full of children in the back, all the windows down, smiles in full beam. His clothes didn't look nice or feel right, and as he got aboard the bus he felt on display for the passengers. By the time the bus reached their neighborhood, they were standing cramped near the back, their nets bunched together between them. When he spoke at her, it was through a kind of scrim, her features blurred like at confessional.

"Soon we won't be able to do this as often," he said.

She was staring at the Tawny Emperor.

"I know," she said.

"I'll miss it," he said. And then: "I'll miss you."

She didn't look up. He wasn't sure if she heard.

* * *

Some fathers took for their daughters and sons great pains. They dug into the earth and they felled trees to make a home stand warm, and they pushed themselves to beat a child when in her carelessness she broke a tool or heirloom. It couldn't be easy. Hadn't that been the truth for his father, a man who'd won his son's love through fear and awe? He would soon, he knew, be a father himself, and he worked more hours than he could bear so that this little thing could grow on its own by having at hand whatever was needed. Warm socks. Encyclopedias. An upright piano on a stable floor. A father to count on. It took effort to become this man, the rapid pace of the factory always a threat. He cut his boards slower than most but quick enough not to draw wrath from the supervisor, and over time his reputation at the factory had become meager. He worked, they'd decided, on the lazy side of competent, and because he'd never rise any ranks he took on every shift, always worried about becoming a charity case. One morning the man at the bandsaw with a bushy moustache that filled with sawdust each shift pulled from his jacket pocket a short pine board. The man looked furtively to each side and caught his eye. "Little something for the little lady," he said. "Don't tell the boss." The board wasn't much longer than his own hand, and as he watched the man bend over the bandsaw, its blade chugging and ravenous, he thought about love and what it made men do. Then he heard a yelp, saw the board kick and go flying into a dusty corner, and this man, this conspirator, staggered backward, one hand holding another soaked red. From this close he could see the extent of it: sawn right through at the palm.

That night he returned moody and hungry, and when he sat at the kitchen table he looked down on a plate of creamed cabbage over toast. She was over in the reading chair, maybe fifteen feet away, watching him, he could tell. He didn't want to look at her, so he ate quickly, the whole plate clear in seven bites. "Is there more?"

"There's mine," she said. "I haven't had mine yet."

He pushed the plate away, the fork clattering to the floor. He wanted to talk about what he saw at the factory that morning but would never.

"I work hard," he said. "I get so hungry it hurts. And this is all I get." He got up from the table and the metal chair's legs ground and squealed against the floor. She also stood, to start counterbalancing his movements.

"There's no money for more," she said. "I'm sorry. I try to make it seem like more. The toast."

"I pick up three extra shifts a week," he said. "That's a hamburger steak. Chicken and dumplings." He was standing with his back to her at the sink, rinsing out his glass, worried about crushing the thing. "You give me cabbage. How am I supposed to have any energy tomorrow?"

She had to back up to keep from falling, all the way to the fireplace. "But I keep gaining weight," she said, almost yelling to be heard over the sound of running water. "And this house. It's getting harder and harder. . . ." She didn't know how to finish.

He turned around and strode quickly toward her, his boots heavy on the floor like a pirate's. "So this is my fault, is it? That I'm too heavy? That I can't fix the problem?"

She tried to get as near to him as possible. "We could be the same size, for a while."

He kept moving past her, all the way to the front door, forcing her to scramble into the kitchen. They heard the angry moans of the house as it tempered itself to their actions. He went out to the backyard and scrambled into the crawlspace, and he grabbed the closest shotgun and a box full of shells, and he moved out to the side of the house. Using his eyes to measure the midpoint in the foundation, he sighted it along the barrel and pulled the trigger. He heard his wife scream inside, a wail that shivered his cold skin, and he heard the house shudder with the blow. He shot again and saw his wife running toward him from the right. "Stop it!" she cried. "Stop it! Stop!"

He opened the barrel to remove the empty shells. He could see the lights from the street reflected in his wife's wet eyes and it made him feel shameful. She was trembling, and he was surprised to find that he was as well. He couldn't say anything, so he simply dropped the gun on the ground and headed up to bed.

That night they lay apart, a body's width between them, and sometime before he dreamed heard a voice.

—She'll never stay still.

It had the thin, snarling voice of creaking floorboards. He felt it right in his ears.

—What do you mean? he asked it.

—You won't always be able to hold her. But I can.

He thought of rolling over and taking her in his arms right now, but he didn't want to wake her.

—Not her, the voice said. The baby.

And then it was as though he were given a dream. He saw himself and his wife standing apart in the house, the baby now grown into a walking toddler. Indeed: a girl. She clambered over the floor with a burning curiosity, and he and his wife moved like sportsmen to keep everything in balance. The baby looked old enough to talk, but she didn't talk. She crawled fiercely, faster than he could follow. He looked over at his wife and saw that she was nude, both of them unaware of how it came to happen. Her expression was pretty, and the body that loomed before him seemed fresh and novel, the body he knew from their wedding night. Her shallow navel. Her long, long legs. Could the house watch her? Could it see?

—I'm not in love with her, it said. Or you.

—What, then?

The house didn't say anything, but in the dream he felt the floor rise slowly below him. He watched as his wife sank down and away, stumbling a little in the shift of balance. The baby was sliding away, too, headed toward the wall. He tried to be heavier. He jumped as hard as he could on the floor and tried to force it back down. He jumped again and again, and he jumped once more and the floor crashed below him, and a large tear ran along the center of the house. He'd split the thing in two. He heard his wife's voice in a heightened shriek. "The baby! Do you have her?" He didn't see the baby. Across the room, the floor rose up to nothing but a jagged edge of torn floorboards. The furniture was massed around him like a pond that he had to wade through. He climbed over it all and up the incline of the floor and peered into the chasm he'd created.

—Stillness, the voice said.

He felt the force of the house draw him closer, and he fell in and he continued to fall.

The next morning was the start of another weekend, and he woke late to an empty bed and the smell of sausages. Downstairs he saw his wife at the stove. Looking around the two rooms, the dream from that night hit him like déjà vu, the house both foreign and familiar. He moved slowly toward the kitchen and she called out to him, feeling him, he guessed, in the motions of the floor.

"I made you some breakfast. Come eat it and maybe afterward we can hang the Tawny Emperor."

She'd fried up a potato, too, and he ate the whole greasy plate of food as slowly as he could, and he savored each bite. This was her apology, this meal for him. Afterward he went around back and crawled under the house. His guns, he noticed, were nowhere to be seen, but the butterfly jar was still on a shelf past the canned vegetables, and just enough light came in through the narrow entry for him to reach and grab onto the specimen, careful not to knock it against the glass and upset the poise of its wings. The Emperor was long dead by now, cleanly suffocated in the ether. On his way back to the house he stopped in the tool shed and selected one of the empty wood-and-glass cases he had made during the winter, one square and wide enough to accommodate the Emperor's majesty.

She sat at the kitchen table and carefully pinned the specimen in place, and he sat on the hearth, getting his tools in order. Hammer, nails, level. There wasn't a table near the wall that he could set anything on, and his wife would have to stay in the kitchen during the procedure, so he'd need to perform a kind of juggling act, keeping nails in his mouth or the level tucked into an armpit. When she was ready, they met in the doorway and she passed the case to him, standing in place to watch him hang it. "I think I'm rather proud of that catch," she said, a little dreamily. "I wasn't even expecting it. It just showed up right when I was looking in its direction. It was almost too perfect to be luck. Dear? Do you know what I mean? Isn't there a word for that? Isn't it 'serendipity'?"

"I don't know," he mumbled, two nails poking out between his lips like fangs. "Move back a little, the house isn't level."

She did as she was told, standing next to the big empty china cabinet. He held the level steadily above the frame of the specimen's case and made light scratches in the wall where the two nails should go. Scratch, scratch, about four inches apart. He put the case and level down at his feet and began setting the first nail into the wall. The plaster was thick and stubborn, much like the house, and he pounded heavily with the hammer as though to hurt it. He drove harder and harder, filling the room with this noise, until he heard another cutting through it like an alarm.

"Dear," his wife yelled. "Dear, come quick."

He stopped hammering. "What?"

"The baby's kicking," she said. "Quick. Come feel."

He held the other nail up to the scratch mark. "I can't. I'll lose the mark and have to do this all over again."

So early, he thought. The house was right. He wouldn't be able to hold on. He positioned the second nail and felt a sudden shift in the floor, and there was his wife right behind him.

"Here," she said, and she grabbed his hand. "Before it stops."

He startled, and with the leaning of the house he lost his balance and fell. The case fell with him, and glass shattered across the floor. "Get back!" he yelled at her. "Go back to the doorway!"

"But, dear," she said. She knelt down to him and the house tilted even more. Furniture began sliding toward them. From the floor, he almost wanted to kick her, like he would a mule. Get her to move away from him. He heard her yelp a little, and he saw the coffee table leaning into the back of her legs.

"Go, damn you!" he yelled again.

She listened this time and ran toward the kitchen, tripping over the edge of the davenport, which had slid five feet out from the wall. She fell into the kitchen, landing on her stomach, and then she looked up and screamed, ducking her head beneath her arms.

"Are you okay?" he said. "What is it?"

She looked up. He couldn't see what she looked up at.

"The china cabinet," she said. "It's going to fall."

He stood up to take a look.

"No!" she screamed. She prayed he'd stay still.

"It's going to fall on us."

In the mayhem, the cabinet had somehow toppled over, getting caught by two kitchen chairs. On the floor, she faced the enormous object, its wide glass panels just feet from her head. Her belly. The baby had stopped kicking, and her right ankle burned. Something awful had happened to it in the fall from the davenport. She looked over at her husband and she told him not to move. The kitchen chairs wouldn't hold for long and she didn't know where to go to save herself. She watched him disobey her, stooping to gather the pieces of glass, and then he swore and threw the case across the room, sucking at his finger. "I cut myself," he said, and it was what he deserved, her reckless husband. And what about her? This house, she'd worked so hard to make it a home when it was more like an arena where they played out these endless battles. The case had landed next to her on the floor, the Emperor's wings torn and bent in cruel angles. She announced it ruined, and across the house her husband had sat back down, directly underneath the Marble Warlock. "I'm sorry," he said, looking at his hands. The floor was still at a tilt. She knew she needed to get further away from him, but she was afraid to move. Her ankle in agony now. She had to find the strength, and she waited to feel another kick, another sign of that life inside. The cabinet hovered in the air above her.

Little Fingers

1.

Even given all the stuff that happened, I've never blamed Joyce. Joyce was this hilarious, angry lady who wore flats every day and was much smaller than me and had just permanent greeny eye bags, but she liked my organizing talents and my work ethic and smoked cigarettes with me and only me after lunch. Joyce kept everything running. She would have told me to get over it, and I think by now I have.

I remember when she hired me, stealing me from the team who put together the WQED Pittsburgh Community Calendar visuals and setting me up in the production room to help control the look of *Dig In with Calvin Woolfe,* the cooking show she'd already brought to the top of our ratings after just one season. I started on a Friday morning and she sat me in my cubicle and stood in my entryway and raised her voice. "Okay, Ginny," she said. We were almost at eye level to each other. "The show needs better captions.

Show me what you've got on Monday." She turned around and there was her office, where the door got shut and I didn't see her the rest of the day.

I ignored David all weekend to find the look I wanted, staying glued to the tube for inspiration, and Sunday evening just before prime time this commercial came on TNN for Nose Better, and the captions like "Non-Greasy" and "Moisturized" and "Penetrating Vapors" scrolled in from the top right corner and landed in the lower middle of the screen. But skewed, on the diagonal. The tone was a muted pink. The words were in a serif font, like in books. Everything about it was counterintuitive. Mr. Davidson was my graphic design teacher at Carnegie Mellon, and because American eyes moved naturally left to right he'd shout in class for us to guide the eye—"GUIDE THE EYE!"—while we sliced poster board with our X-Actos. The captions in the Nose Better commercial, it was like throwing words at people's faces. Our show was hosted by a man with a restaurant downtown named the Bay and Howl, and to me captions like those would be the perfect match for Chef Calvin's extreme personality.

Monday morning I showed Joyce my sketches and explained the whole concept. "No way in hell are we putting anything on a diagonal," she said.

I asked if maybe we could still sweep them in from right to left.

"No way in hell. Just put the captions on the screen, Ginny."

I got to keep the serif font, though. That much she gave me.

Episodes got taped on Thursdays and were broadcast on Sundays. I'd been there almost a week before I got to meet Calvin Woolfe, who shook my hand and told me to call him "just Chef Cal." We were standing by his hand-rinsing sink. Calvin Woolfe had arrived in costume, a pressed chef's jacket buttoned to the throat and this blooming pair of zebra-striped pants. No hat. He stood as tall as a soda machine in front of me, and the blacks and greys and whites of his hair all seemed to be fighting one another, and I couldn't help notice that the forearms exposed under his jacket's rolled-up sleeves were dark and furry, like the backs of exotic bugs. Nathaniel, the production assistant in charge of Calvin Woolfe's needs, was nibbling on the rounded edge of his clipboard and prancing about on his tippy-toes; he needed to go over Calvin's lines. But I needed to keep the man around for a little while, so I asked him if he had any pets.

"I've got pet peeves," he said.

Those arms were folded up across his chest and he was bowing over a little to speak, I imagine, more intimately toward me. But then Calvin turned to his assistant before I could ask any more questions. "I need lip balm and cigarettes."

Nathaniel flew off as though punted into the shadows of the studio, and Calvin strolled after him. "Gina?" he called out. "A pleasure."

I didn't mind that he fucked up my name. People are hard of hearing sometimes. I was a professional woman now with her own phone extension and I had a job to do. During taping, I'd sit on a squeaky rolling stool in the production booth with Joyce, waiting for her to give me the camera cues. It was button-punching work, mostly—the only, like, "uplifting" part coming from those rare times I could let go of my drama enough to just merge with Joyce's whole person, so that when she, staring savagely at her monitors with those headphones Princess Leia'd around her gorgeous hair, called out to get ready for camera two, I was already there, my right index finger poised over camera two's little green button.

Taping ended around three and Joyce's "That's a wrap, people" always also meant for the workday. It was a reward every week and I took the extra time to walk home, even on cold days. The building that housed WQED's TV-radio-print empire was right on the residential edge of Oakland, right where the neighborhood got tony, and these were the homes I'd have to walk past to get to our Bloomfield row house. On that stretch of Fifth Avenue where the mansions were corralled like enormous beasts behind wrought-iron fences, I'd slow to a drunkard's shuffle. They had names, these houses, and circular drives that ran underneath carports near the kitchen. It's where we'd tell the pizza guy to come. By the time I got to our dinky brick thing it was usually past 6 PM. Maybe I'd stop in a shop or two, or grab a slice at Angelo's. Every time, David would ask if taping went late, and every time I'd say yes.

It became a routine, but I've always liked routines. Fridays I wrote and printed all the captions for the previous day's episode. The names of the idiots who worked the cameras and lit the set, people like Nathaniel, took no time at all. The hard part was listing the ingredients for Calvin Woolfe's recipes. That first episode I worked on, he made a chicken fricassee and I watched the tape with Post-Its on my desk, jotting *1 whl chx 3–4 1b, 1 yll O chpd, 1 red pep chpd, 1 grn pep chpd.* But once all the chopped food was thrown together and Calvin made the gravy, the ingredients became lazy and curious stabs at flavor. "Let's toss in some cumin," he said, "and a little bit of coriander. And you know what, folks, what the heck, throw in all the cayenne pepper you want. But hey, be careful." He pointed at the camera. "This ain't baby food!" I rewound and replayed, looking to see how much was "some" and whether "some" was more or less than "a little bit." I rewound and replayed. I heard Calvin Woolfe say "baby food!" thirteen times, watched him grin like a blackjack winner thirteen times, felt pinned down and accused by thirteen index fingers pointing right between my eyes. Then I went to ask Joyce.

"Vince just guessed when he did it," she said. "Print whatever makes sense."

I chuckled. "Oh, *sure*. What do I know about cooking?"

"About as much as I do. Go ask Nathaniel, if you need to."

"Do you have Chef Cal's contact info?" I asked.

Joyce grabbed the alarm clock off her desk and held it up in my direction, and she clicked one of her painted fingernails against the front plastic of it. 11:33. "I need those captions in twenty-seven minutes, Ginny. How many minutes?"

"Twenty-seven, ma'am."

"You have twenty-seven minutes to figure it out for yourself."

At home one night, I had David quiz me.

"We don't even have cumin," he said. "What would we do with cumin?"

"Just use whatever." I sat at the kitchen table with my back to him, smoking a cigarette and trying not to peek. "Use sugar or even coffee. But don't let me see you!"

I heard him rifle through the utensil drawer. In the other room, the TV had been turned off and the lights throughout the house were dark. Sometimes I tried to look at our house from the street while I and David were living inside. I gave us see-through walls, like a dollhouse. I made up stories about the figures who lived there. *Are they happy, these two? Let's watch what they do next.*

"You want me to just hand you some?" David said.

"Put it in a bowl. I'll guess how much it is."

"I thought we talked about never bringing work home."

Back then, I felt that David was holding me away from something I almost had in my grasping hands. I've always been a look-forwarder. Here I was with this just great new job, and here he was bringing up old college promises I could barely remember making. "Did I agree to that?" I asked.

"Ginny, I don't want to do this," he said and walked out into the darkness of the house. *Quitter.* I quizzed myself, using my fingers to pull from the coffee can whatever I thought a tablespoon was, whatever an eighth of a teaspoon could possibly be. I tried to do a cup, but it wasn't even a whole single fistful. It was more like four fists.

Proud, I told Joyce all about it the next day.

"Wonderful, Ginny," she said, shining her desk's nameplate with the elbow of her cardigan, "but the only people who copy these recipes down are old-folks-homers dying in front of their sets. Who cooks stewed lamb for eight?"

She was Joyce, she knew her demographics. But still I took the job seriously. What other proper document existed? Calvin hadn't written a cookbook. The Internet wasn't around yet. The hundreds of tapes that filled the shelves in WQED's basement were the only testament to Calvin Woolfe's artistry, and I was like his Moses, maybe, etching him into stone.

One Thursday I knocked on the greenroom door wearing jeans and some old T-shirt. "It's open," Calvin yelled. I pushed my way in. He was there with Nathaniel, who sat bent up at the makeup table with his legs crossed, eating noodles from a carton. The room was small and flooded by low fluorescents. It had no windows. Cigarette smoke fell over my face.

"What can I do for you?" Calvin said, stripped to the waist in those zebra pants he always wore. A clear glass ashtray rested on his paunch like a diamond on some velvety pillow.

I smiled, bashful in his unbashfulness. I asked if he could maybe be more exact on the show. With the ingredients.

"You have a problem with my cooking?" he asked.

Nathaniel held his chopsticks in the air like a little set of rabbit ears.

"No, no!" I said. "It's just that I never know exactly what quantities to put in. For the captions?"

Calvin Woolfe stared at me for a moment, smoking.

"On the screen?"

"Gina, this is *cooking*," he said, stubbing out his cigarette. "It's not your math homework." Then he stood, and in that tiny room he took up so much space that no matter how I moved my arm I felt it would land somewhere on his body.

"Time to get dressed," Nathaniel said, appearing suddenly between us. He was holding up Calvin's chef's jacket.

"It was real nice talking with you," Calvin said, shrugging both big shoulders into his clothes.

I took him to mean the measurements didn't matter and taught myself how to read him, keeping my eyes on Calvin's hammy hands as they dipped knives into slabs of butter or drizzled oil from a cruet. It was easy to pretend that everything he said into the camera he was saying to me. After all, I got him first, every week. By the time the rest of Pittsburgh saw Chef Cal cook my eyes had been all over him, and my captions had been placed on the screen like a fence he couldn't climb over.

2.

Then a lot of things happened very quickly. Around the six-week mark I saw Calvin Woolfe walk into Joyce's office, and Calvin never showed on Mondays. Minutes later, they walked out of Joyce's office. Joyce dipped her head into my cubicle. "Can you join us in the conference room for a minute?" There I was introduced to Nicole Slayton, head of communications for WQED. We shook hands. Her skirt's hem hung close to her privates, and she kept her hair short, too. It sat on her head like a bunch of dead kelp. When she offered her hand to Calvin he pressed his lips to it, and we all sat down around the table. WQED wanted to publish Calvin's first cookbook, culled from two seasons of *Dig In with Calvin Woolfe,* and this meeting, Nicole explained, was to get everyone's heads together. "Joyce, let's start with you," she said. "Any ideas?"

"Call Rebecca over at the magazine and get her to start running a column every month with one of Cal's recipes," she said. "And maybe some kitchen tips. We need to build an audience first."

Nicole scribbled some words in her leather-bound notebook. "That's a fantastic idea."

"Let's talk *cover*," Calvin said. "Is it going to be a picture of my food, or do you want it to be a picture of me?"

Calvin started grinning all up at Nicole and she leered in and grinned back, and it was like they were going to make out right there in front of poor Joyce. "Whatever you're comfortable with," Nicole said.

"Oh, I'm comfortable with whatever you're comfortable with."

"What's my involvement in this book?" I asked. I tried to look everyone in the eye, like conspiratorially. "I mean, where's Nathaniel?"

Nicole explained that I was to help cull recipes. "We figured the easiest way to generate copy would be to go to the episodes, take from the ingredient lists. That way there's also some consistency."

Calvin prepared four dishes during each episode and we shot twenty-four episodes a season. That made 192 recipes I'd have to translate into on-paper instructions, and I didn't know then what I know now. I thought Calvin Woolfe would have to help. I imagined late Thursday afternoons over coffee and my notes. I imagined small, intimate tables tucked in the corners of bars, away from all those display windows up front.

"But surely," I said to Nicole Slayton's face, "Chef Cal has recipes I should borrow from?"

"To be honest, Gina, I don't really write much down," Calvin Woolfe said to me.

"Jesus, Cal, her name's Ginny," Joyce said. "You just heard it a few seconds ago."

"But that's short for Gina, right?" I watched him wiggle a finger in his ear.

Nicole laughed like this was a joke and gave us, gave *me*, a three-month deadline. "Let's make this book great, everyone," she said and the meeting was over. What a ditz, I thought and watched Calvin hold the door open for Nicole. As she passed through he shook his head once and it was clear he was looking at her flat ass. He followed after her. I had to completely grab the doorknob and pull it all the way open again for Joyce.

I spent extra hours on Tuesday and Thursday digging through the archives, finding the typewritten transcripts we were required by law to provide the deaf or VCR-less in order to cull the instructions on how long to stick things in the oven or when to add new vegetables to the pot. My job became joining my professional voice with Calvin's enthusiastic one, so that when he said, "What you want to do is take that pie crust and just toss the thing on there. Just throw it right on. Get messy, people! It's a pot pie, not a wedding cake!" I wrote, *Lay crust over bowl. It's O.K. if it looks uneven.* Lots of times the work got boring. It was hard to spend time with a man whose food I never got to eat, so one night I stopped about halfway through the fourth episode of the first season, and when I got home at five I told David we should go out for dinner.

"All right," he said, wiping his small hands on a rag. "I could use a break." We were down in the basement, where David did all his refinishing work. Over in the corner I could see that the previous day's rainfall had leaked in and formed a puddle on the floor, but I was too excited to let it get to me.

I suggested the Bay and Howl.

"That'll be expensive," David said. "Will that guy give you a discount, do you think?"

"I'm not going to ask him for a discount, David. Are you serious?"

"All right, all right. Let me go change."

"Oh, you look fine," I said. "Let's just go now before the rush."

"I've got stains on my pants," he said.

I told him no one was going to notice.

The Bay and Howl was dark inside, like a den, with tables you could tell were heavy and a thick carpet underfoot I felt I could lie down and curl up on if I wanted to. And I really wanted to. We were seated right next to a big fish aquarium, and through its bluey glass I could see the doors to the kitchen waver like a mirage.

David took forever. "What's pesto?" he asked. "Is it sweet?"

"Just order it," I said. "This is like some kind of *adventure*, right?"

The waiter brought us a basket of pencil-thin breadsticks, which David began chomping on, and I asked whether Calvin was going to be making our dinners.

"Chef Cal has a personal investment in every dish that leaves his kitchen," the boy said.

And I just clapped my hands then. "Oh, how righteous!"

David snapped another breadstick in half. "Don't you see this guy, like, every week?"

"He's very busy in the studio," I said and explained all the new work I had to do for the cookbook.

"They paying you extra for that?"

"That's not the point," I said and listened instead to that great rumble of polite conversation and knives on dinner plates. Our food came and it was delicious. "Can you tell Calvin Woolfe that we said so?" I asked the waiter as he cleared our plates. "And we'd like to pay our compliments directly?" The boy nodded and took off for the busing station.

"Let's just go home, okay?" David said. "I want to finish that dresser tonight."

"I bet a place like this has the newspaper framed on the wall," I said. "Go check."

And suddenly we were arguing, right in front of a stuffed bear. On its hind legs! David kept saying things about *purpose*—his *purpose* in life and the *purpose* of marriage in life. It all got a little confused, I thought, and I told him so.

"Don't tell me I'm confused, Ginny," he said.

"I didn't say *you* were confused, I said—"

"And don't throw semantic arguments at me," he said. "You can't run from this problem. I am unhappy with this marriage and you are, too."

"Oh, now who's putting words in whose mouth?"

"You work late. You spend hours every weekend shopping. You sit alone in that kitchen because you'd rather do anything than spend time with me. And maybe I'm the same way with my projects in the basement, but isn't that a sign? All those promises we made in college. Remember?"

I didn't know what he was talking about, and as he kept ranting I found a little cockleshell at the bottom of the aquarium and slid myself underneath it.

"You're not even listening to me," David said.

I kept my voice at a whisper. "I can't believe you're bringing all this up right now. Right here around all these people."

"I want to see a therapist."

"Then go," I said.

"I want *us* to go."

And I said no way was I going to spend money on some shrink to tell me what I was feeling.

And he said he couldn't be with somebody who wouldn't even try to be with somebody.

And then he was gone from the table.

Oh, David. In college you named a robot after me, even though all it did was scuttle clumsily over low debris. It was enough to make me fall for you, back then. But then right after we got married you turned all serious and became this strange burden in the house. The only things we talked about were home improvement and vacation planning. We weren't even thirty! Since when did sharing our lives together mean giving them up completely?

I sat there for the next hour, undisturbed. Where else was I going to go? No one came to refill my glass of water, so I kept my eyes fixed on the surfboard-shaped window between the restaurant and the kitchen, waiting for Calvin Woolfe to walk past. I didn't see him until after the restaurant closed. His bimbo hostess pointed at my table, and through his aquarium's glass Calvin looked over at me like a frightened little fish. But then he smiled once he recognized me, and he came over to the table.

"You've been waiting all this time," he said.

"The food was so good, Calvin."

He said that was kind and asked if I wanted to see the kitchen. I jumped right out of my chair. He showed me the walk-in cooler, the place where all the knives were kept, and the hook outside his office where he hung his chef's hat. There was no one else around. I told him of my plan to get a taste of his food so I could write about it better. I said I wanted to try *all* his dishes. He invited me into his office and closed the door behind me. I suppose this was what I'd waited all night for, but I'm not one of those slutty girls who sleeps her way to the top. That was never my intention. But when he put his enormous hands on those problem spots at my waist, I didn't make any kind of protest. It was like being held by a sycamore tree. It was nice, at first. But then he kind of threw me on his desk and my head banged against his Rolodex, which really hurt. "Fuck yeah, whore," he said when I moaned, and I wasn't sure I heard him right. *Fuck there more?* I felt his fist in my hair, and he pulled and kept talking. "Yeah bitch, little bitch." And, "Get on that horse-cock, get the fuck on it." And suddenly I wasn't having a good time.

"You don't have to be a shit about it," I said, coughing, trying to get comfortable.

And suddenly I'd fallen onto the floor.

"You think I need some cunt telling me how to fuck her?" he said. I started gathering my clothes. "Little girl, you hang around my restaurant all night, you take what I fucking give you."

"I only wanted—"

"Get the fuck. Out of my office."

All *punctuated* like that. I had to walk back to the house by myself that night through some neighborhoods I avoided even in the light of day. I could have been raped, or murdered. When I got home the lights in the living room were still lit, and I found some lies inside me to tell David about what happened. *Those spring rolls didn't sit right and I had to walk into three separate Eckerds before I found some medicine that cost less than the five dollars I had in my pocket.* But I didn't find David in the living room when I walked in, and I didn't find him in bed, either. I couldn't find him anywhere in the house, actually. I fell asleep on my own.

3.

The season ended in June, and by that time I'd finished every damn recipe and sent them to Nicole. It was out of my hands now. The book ran quickly through the printing process, to be out in time for WQED's end-of-the-summer pledge drive. In the mean-time, work on the show was scarce and unstructured, and Joyce and I took long lunches in Oakland or even the South Side, when we felt adventurous. I don't live there anymore, Pittsburgh, but when I did it felt as though I were stuck in some gigantic rut, like geophysically. We lived in a place where all the winds and water in the sky collided and sat moodily amid the hills. What I mean is, a Pittsburgher sees more grey skies than blue, so when the sun came out everyone wanted to just eat it up. Like we were all walking trees, reaching our limbs up high above us.

One afternoon, Joyce and I were taking the long way back after an al fresco lunch on South Craig. She was talking about the *Dig In* column, which had been running in the magazine for four or five months at that point. "They got a letter from some old kook," she said. "Says all the recipes taste terrible."

"I haven't tried them," I said. We were both walking up Flagstaff Hill, where couples young and old lay close on bright-colored blankets, and all the pale boys had their shirts off, as though in contest with one another.

"This guy claims his spaghetti Bolognese was swimming in sauce."

"Wasn't it swimming in sauce on the show?" I asked, trying to remember. "I don't know why Calvin can't write them down himself."

"The man can't even read, Ginny," she said. "We can't expect him to write a thank-you note, much less a whole magazine column."

I thought she was kidding. I laughed because I thought she was just kidding.

"Of course I have no proof of this, so you'll keep your mouth shut about it."

"Oh, my god! How do you know?" I asked, my hand covering that mouth, practicing.

"He won't use cue cards," she said. "Nathaniel handles all the paperwork."

Such secrets! At that moment it was like Joyce had given me the best gift on my bridal registry.

"Wow," I said. "I mean, who's illiterate these days?"

"Who cares?" she said. "The point is I don't want any more letters about failed recipes."

I told her maybe there was a typo somewhere, but what I
wanted to tell her was that no way could it have been my fault. I'd
worked hard to make sure all the things Calvin Woolfe did with
food and his hands became something anybody could follow, word
for word. *My* words. But Joyce liked action, not excuses, so I nodded instead, like I understood what she was talking about.

Back at the office, Joyce had an envelope on her desk—small
and squarish and white. It could have fit into her pocket.

"Ah," she said. "An invitation to the book release."

But I hadn't gotten one!

"Calm down, Cinderella," she said, reading my face like a cue
card. "You can come with me."

The party was held in the restaurant at the top of the USX Tower, about a thousand feet up in the air. Joyce said she'd meet me
there, but as I stepped off the elevator I couldn't find her, or anyone
in charge of gate-crashers, so I walked right in. The place was nice
but ugly. Salmon-colored walls and a kind of sea-foam green tint
to the patterned carpet. I felt like I was standing at the bottom of
a bowl of unripe vegetables.

Calvin was surrounded by a crowd of snobs, with leggy Nicole
from communications glued to him. Unprofessionally, I thought.
I found the buffet table by the north wall of windows and filled
my plate with what I recognized as Calvin's recipes. Mini spinach-
mushroom quiches. Chicken satay skewers. Grilled eggplant rolls.
I wanted to check whether I could see my house from here, but
it was nighttime and through the windows all I saw were blips
of streetlights peeking through the trees, my own face reflected
dimly back at me. I felt like the tallest woman in Pittsburgh. David
was out there somewhere, maybe. *Incommunicado*, as they said in

the movies. I tried not to get melodramatic about it, but what was he waiting for? All my messages left with his secretary had gone unreturned.

Nathaniel walked past with a copy of the book in his hand, and I saw he was wearing the exact same terra cotta blazer I was, which made me feel as ugly as the restaurant. So I resolved to leave and pick up a whole pizza at Angelo's, but as I turned to go Joyce was right there with an empty glass in her hand. "Have you tried the food?" she asked.

I'd been enjoying the chicken satay, but the peanut sauce wasn't very good. "I just can't taste the peanuts," I said, and it was true. It was like dipping chicken into a sticky broth made from more chicken.

"Everything sucks," she said. "Pardon my French."

"Who's catering the party?" I wondered. I saw over Joyce's low head that Nathaniel and Calvin were huddled by the restrooms, flipping quickly through the pages of the cookbook as though it were some porno mag one of them had found. Except their eyes weren't hornily wide open. They were thin and irritated.

"This place is so ugly," Joyce said. Was she drunk?

And that's when Calvin came over with Nathaniel in tow. I watched them stomp through the crowd with their arms swinging, like two toughs storming into a saloon. "A quarter cup of peanuts?" Calvin said. "A teaspoon of sugar? A tablespoon of cilantro? Where'd you get these measurements?"

"From the show," I said. I remembered the episode perfectly. It was the one he'd filmed after telling me that cooking wasn't math. I'd watched him prepare the peanut sauce at least three times, live and on tape. "You chopped the peanuts and threw in a whole handful," I said, as though he weren't there.

"A whole handful?" he said, and he grabbed my hand and held it in the air between us.

It looked like a big fish swallowing a little one.

"We trusted you with Calvin's recipes," Nathaniel said. "*We trusted you.*"

The partygoers were starting to look our way, I could tell. Joyce wouldn't come in and defend me for some reason.

"My name wasn't even included in the book!" I said, looking at Joyce. "I wasn't even given any *credit.*"

"And it's a fucking shame," Calvin said. "You think I want my name attached to this? These aren't my recipes."

And that was true. They weren't. They were *my* recipes. Calvin was just a face. I could have done everything he'd wanted. I could have lain my body down on the floor at his every prompting. I could have cut off all my hair for him and he'd still have treated me like a burden. It was like long ago he'd planned out this life for himself, this mini-celebrity he was now starting to enjoy in town, and that plan didn't include anyone else. I wondered how Nathaniel put up with it, and it was only then as I left the party that I felt sorry for the boy.

I spent Saturday in bed, and Sunday in the paper I read all about the book release party in the society column. All the hyphenated names in boldface, once again mine nowhere to be found. I was there, though, buried in polite allusion. "A moment early on when Chef Cal let loose that fiery spirit he's known for all around town didn't put a damper on this sky-high fête. And the food? *Tres délicieux!*" Which was kind, unlike the review of the book itself, which ran with a headline—"Woolfe 'Digs' Own Grave with Howl-Worthy Book"—I had to admit was clever.

I resolved to make things better and spent that Sunday evening skipping TV and going through my copy of *Dig In* recipe-by-recipe, underlining the measurements I'd probably guessed at. I kept thinking of his fist, Calvin's, shaking my own fist in front of my face. From what I could tell, his was between one and one-third and one and one-half times bigger than mine, and I thought if we could perform that same operation on the ingredients we could release a second edition, maybe with photographs to make it more attractive.

I came in Monday with the timeline planned out in a notebook. I felt it was very professional and that Joyce would be proud, but Joyce wasn't in her office when I walked in. I thought maybe she was having a pee, and I sat down and checked my phone messages. But I didn't have any messages. And then Nicole Slayton was standing behind me with Mike from HR and Don Mooney, the president of WQED, who wore a deep blue suit and stood about two me's side by side. He was smiling so kindly that I was confused at first when I heard Mike tell me to pack up all my things. That I had to leave the building because I was no longer employed by the company.

"We're sorry, Virginia, but this cookbook fiasco's set the company back a few dollars," Nicole said.

"Eighty thousand dollars," Mr. Mooney said. "And I don't need to tell you that for a nonprofit weathering the storm of a recession that's suicide money."

The weird thing was that I didn't even cry, and I always cry when people gang up on me.

People who wrote letters to the editor always came across to me as tired old coots who had nothing in life except a chance to get the last word in. That man who wrote in about how awful my recipes were, for instance. But when I got home from work I got some paper from David's office and sat down at his desk. It was the first time I'd stepped foot in the room since he left. Why David needed an office I never understood, but here were all the things about himself he loved. That ancient Selectric he wrote all his

college papers on. A steel T-square. A Kennywood mug: **DAVID**.
The only light in the room came from a lamp on the desk I sat at,
and it felt exactly like being at the very back end of some cave. If
I had swirled around in his chair I wouldn't have been able to see
the front wall, but I knew what was there. I could close my eyes
and see the framed photograph of me from sophomore year lying
on the grass in the quad, my sweatshirt riding up and showing
the outie I had back then. And my hair? A stupid, sticky mess of
hairspray. I'd done so much work over the years to make it natural-
looking, but did David ever think to take a new picture? The whole
wall was like some kind of shrine to this older version of me. The
thinner version.

My letter was ten pages long, but by the time I typed it up and
did some cutting I got it down to two, double-spaced. I signed it in
pen and folded it into an envelope and drove it right down to the
offices of the *Post-Gazette* and set it at the security desk. That was
at 11:30. I was in bed by twelve.

That's probably the end of my story. It took me a long time to
find another job, and even longer to find another husband. The
Post-Gazette, though, was quick and printed my letter that Friday, and though I checked each day, no letters ever followed in
response. I thought maybe Calvin Woolfe would have something
to add. I thought he'd want the last word. I'm sure Nathaniel
would've read it for him.

Sometime on Saturday I was in the kitchen adding salt to a pan
of onions and garlic when I heard the doorbell. I didn't want to
disturb my cooking. In the previous week I'd tried to get outside
and get some sun, and I took out a ton of money from savings and
spent it all at the grocery store, stocking up the pantry, buying
produce I'd never tried before, breads that didn't come sealed in
a plastic bag. Maybe I'd been trying to avoid the heavy envelope

that had come in the mail, marked with the letterhead of David's lawyer, but every day I'd stood around the kitchen making whatever I felt like making on the stove. I had one rule: no cookbooks. Lots of what I ended up with was awful. I remember boiling a lamb chop before slicing it into a stir-fry. I just tossed it out and tried something else, what did I care? When the doorbell rang I didn't even know what I was going to do with my sautéed onions and garlic—oh, I had all the terms down—but I knew I was going to add either mushrooms or broccoli rabe, and as I was trying to decide the doorbell rang again and then again. I said, "Okay!" and shut off the heat.

It was Nathaniel, leaning against the outside stoop rail with a copy of Friday's newspaper in his hands.

"Bravo, Ginny," he said. "Fucking *great* letter."

"Oh, what do you want?" I said. He was drunk. It wasn't even noon!

"I want Chef Cal's cookbook back!" He shouted this, and I thought I heard it reverberate off the houses across from me, so I ushered him inside and asked if I could get him some coffee.

"I was the true author of that cookbook," he said, reading from my letter. *"The idea behind the dishes might be Mr. Woolfe's, but the recipes themselves are my own. If they have any faults, they're my fault.* A little too late, don't you think?"

"I thought I should set the record straight," I said. "I didn't want people to think he was a bad chef."

Nathaniel flopped down on the sofa, putting his shoes up on the armrest. "People *know* he's a great chef."

"It wasn't even really my fault," I said.

He closed his eyes and rubbed fiercely at them with his fists. "I know you think of me as some petty faggot, Ginny."

"I don't!"

"I don't care what you think of me. But you don't know anything. It's clear in your stupid letter. You're not the *author* of the book, okay? You were just the conduit. A set of little fingers. And you've destroyed Calvin's whole career. And because he's my mentor you've destroyed me."

I told him about my plan for a revised version.

"Who cares?" he said, rolling over on his side. Was he going to take a nap? "You never get a second chance to make a first impression," he said. "Even deodorant commercials are smarter than you."

And here I grabbed his two feet and pulled him onto the floor. "I'm not going to let you talk to me like that in my *house*, Nathaniel. This is my *house!*"

"All right, all right," he said, heading toward the door.

"Why have you been drinking this early?" I asked.

"They fired me, too," he said. "They said my relationship to Calvin had become unprofessional."

This was sad, really, because Nathaniel was so dedicated, and I told him I thought so.

"Well, now we've both been fucked, haven't we?" he said.

At the door he dropped the paper and told me to keep it, which I did, even though I'd already put five copies up in David's office.

"What's that smell?" he asked, sniffing at the air like a dog.

I told him what I was making.

"You a cook," he said with a snort. "That's rich."

And maybe it was.

If You Need Me I'll Be Over There

MY BROTHER WAS GETTING MARRIED ON A BEACH IN North Carolina, and I would not be his best man. Nor would our father. That honor, Jarem announced at Christmas dinner, was going to Mike Koblecky, next to whom my brother stood at the latter's wedding earlier that year, and I supposed there was some reciprocity in these matters. Our plates by then were empty, save for my unsuccessful sweet potatoes, and Santa'd brought Mom a dimmer switch for the dining room, so everyone seemed to glow, like on soft-core. Dad broke out the only something fancy he could find: a bottle of Grand Marnier he'd inexplicably been saving through two presidential administrations. It tasted as sweet as the bottle I'd bought last Cinco de Mayo. We sipped and talked about my brother. Was I a groomsman, then? We haven't worked out all the details, Jarem said, one arm around his bride-to-be, who beamed, all teeth.

I have, like, a hundred friends, Shelley said. It's gonna be so hard to say no.

Though Shelley's family had a house at the Jersey shore, my brother'd somehow bullied her into what counted for Mid-Atlantickers as a destination wedding: the Outer Banks. We used to vacation there. I remembered houses on stilts and getting a boogie board at eleven and feeling like a hotshot. One summer the house we'd rented had a crow's nest we'd clamber up to to read the ads for beer specials that trailed behind noisy biplanes, or to watch the sun set behind the Wright Brothers memorial, that fat monolith. It made me want to be a pilot, for a time. Now I was in grad school. To be a filmmaker? I knew that's not exactly how it worked, but I was glad just to read and teach until I could figure it all out. Jarem's June wedding meant I had to teach second summer term Intro to Pop Culture, and thus no break before fall, but such were the sacrifices I'd make for my brother. In turn, he rewarded me with a job officiating the wedding. Shelley's not religious, he told me over the phone, as though we'd ever been. She thought you'd come up with something good.

I was going to be the best: tears like rain on people's faces. I became a minister online and at night started asking my new boyfriend for help. Speak from the heart, Dean said one night, unhelpfully, and then: Will I be invited? I didn't know how to answer, so I ran my hand reassuringly through the hair on his chest and stared out the window at a distant streetlight. I'd come out to my family three years prior, just weeks after I'd finally come out to myself, a fact that'd always baffled Dean. How could I not have known? At eight he knew he'd grow up to share a bed with Superman, whereas I chastely dated three women over twelve years before finally giving in, as I'd understood it, to my weakness. I wasn't supposed to be like that, was how I'd thought of it. It was hard enough being the younger son, and now I had to bear this extra burden? Dean at these moments looked at me like I were one of those swanlike men eunuch'd for opera: You need therapy.

He was right, and I'd found a PhD in Squirrel Hill with long, grey dreadlocks who took student insurance and was eager, in sessions, to tackle my fear of confrontation. You've always got a choice, she'd say. Speak up or shy away. Shy away and you're out of choices. Speak up and you'll get a response. Good or bad, you get to choose what to do next. I wanted her to direct my dissertation. Plus-Ones Only If Married was the policy Jarem and Shelley had come to in order to rein in their guest list. Which for me was no choice at all. *Special dispensation for the reverend?* I texted on RSVP day. Jarem's response: *Sorry. You haven't been dating that long anyway. He'll understand.* I never texted back. He'd sit on my ordained lap if he had to, but my boyfriend was coming to the wedding.

We got to Nags Head at night, the house a seafoam blue beast right on the shorefront, lit up by a swarm of spotlights. Mom gave us a tour of the place in the same terrycloth caftan I remembered from youth, sweeping her hand like a gameshow model at the two dishwashers, fireplace faced in seaglass, and service elevator that hit all three floors and the driveways underneath. The place had six bedrooms and ours was the farthest up the stairs and, from what I could tell, the smallest: twin bunk beds and balloon wallpaper in bright primary colors. It felt like we were at a camp for chronic bedwetters.

Who's down the hall with the queen? I asked.

That's Mike's room, Mom said. His wife's coming in tomorrow.

I call top bunk, Dean said, giving me a look. He set his bag on the bottom bunk.

Mom said, That's the spirit! and left us to unpack.

Check it out, said Dean, pulling from the nightstand drawer a book in red leatherette: *The Illustrated Children's Bible.*

Sorry for the Don't Fuck Our Son setup, I said. It worked that night, both of us beat from travel. The next morning on the beach

I was negligent with sunscreen and burned my back, and later as distant relatives showed up I visibly winced with each embrace. At the rehearsal, Shelley's mom held a clipboard and led the sixteen groomsmen and bridesmaids up and down an aisle she'd traced in the sand with her flip-flop. I stood between them all, looking over the outline she'd given me: BUDDY'S THING was typed near the top, right after SHELLEY UP THE AISLE. My "thing" was some welcomes and thanks I'd scrawled on two cocktail napkins during the flight. Nothing that would move anyone to tears. I was stuck, uninspired. Then, as Dad and Shelley's mom were figuring out music cues, a seagull flew low over the wedding party and shat on the hair of a short, frog-faced woman I hadn't met yet. It's good luck! Shelley insisted, and the groomsmen kept trying to top each other's jokes, and suddenly this bridesmaid standing second to the end became the star of the evening, and I got an idea for my speech.

Burgers and hot dogs off the grill was the night's rehearsal dinner, and on both tiers of back decks I introduced Dean to whomever I could, showing him off in his fitted polo like he were some pedigreed beagle. One great aunt I hadn't seen since my grandfather's funeral said, Who is this? and when I said My boyfriend she backed away as if he'd just puked.

She's old, I said to Dean.

So was Mother Teresa, he said.

You guys don't look boring, a woman said behind us. She was tall and blonde and deeply tan. Her bare arms looked hewn by a chisel. Moira Koblecky, she said.

You're Mike's wife, I said, introducing myself and Dean. She works in the White House, I told him. Don't you?

I do, she said. Last year I even saw the president once.

At the far end of the deck Jarem, Dad, and some groomsmen were grinning around cigars.

And what do you do? Moira asked.

I'm in grad school, I said. Film studies.

I work in pharmaceuticals, Dean said.

You want to direct?

Maybe write? I shrugged. What kind of plan would I have the courage to execute? Max out my credit card on a short I'd take to festivals? Run to Hollywood with a script and no scruples? But what script? What kind of short? My problem was one of relevance. All my life, I'd never seen art that was about me. No books about second-borns who had to fight for attention. No movies about uptight nerds who wouldn't admit they're gay. When my type showed up in stories, we had to change or we got sacrificed—those were the choices—because stories required heroes, however flawed, who people could admire. If I had only myself to make art from, who would ever want to see it?

Moira said she was looking forward to watching me officiate, and then she excused herself over to the cigar party. The sun went down and the sky turned purple and dense, a scrim of clouds blocking out all the stars. When a round of speeches broke out among the wedding party members, Mike urged his wife to toast in his stead. All right, I'll say something, she began, a wineglass hovering toward the betrothed, tiny Shelley like a joey in Jarem's pouch. I barely know the two of you, so I'll just say you make a beautiful couple, I'm really glad to be here, and . . . what the fuck, let's keep drinking.

Cheers all over the house. We were probably waking the neighbors. I opted out of a toast and took Moira's advice to heart. Four beers became seven, I laughed harder at cousins' stories than anyone, and past midnight I leaned into Dean's ear: I want to get naked with you. It was, as come-ons go, wretched, but it had the desired effect. Up in our little room, Dean undid his pants and they dropped right to his ankles, and to my surprise he stood bareassed before me. I took a moment to take in what I felt like I had won, like a grant from some horny benevolent society. The fur on his chest darkened toward the center, making a kind of plus sign around his pecs that I took as an affirmation. Or was it an arrow pointing somewhere? Your dick always looks so *heavy,* I said.

He laughed. You're drunk.

And did I say, Take advantage of me?

The next morning everything became a suspense film I didn't want to be an extra in. Mike and two groomsmen had driven somewhere late and no one had seen them since. Pressures me into marrying him and then gets cold feet as best man, Moira said at the breakfast table. Or maybe he's got a whore down here. He had the rings on him, Jarem added, and then when Mom called to confirm delivery of the cake there was no answer at the bakery. It's 10:30 in the morning! she yelled into the phone. Dean was acting moody, wouldn't meet my eye. His breakfast was all of a bunch of grapes, and he was the first to leave the table, and he was gone by the time I got back to the room. I looked at my suit jacket hanging in the closet and that's when I remembered I'd forgotten dress shoes. The wedding party, it'd been giddily repeated, would be barefoot for the ceremony, but for the officiant this felt unseemly, like a surgeon in jean shorts. I was, maybe, a man of God now. Mom deputized me to swing by the bakery on my hunt for decent shoes, and before I left I went out to the top deck to scour the beach for Dean, but all I saw were families—big striped rental umbrellas and kids in fluorescent swimsuits lugging pails in from the shoreline. I told everyone inside to tell him my whereabouts. Actually, I said, Tell my boyfriend where I've gone, and then I got in the car.

The bakery was closed. The lights were off inside and no one answered my pounding. The sign said Saturday hours were 7–7, but the bakery was definitely closed. There was a pet grooming store next door I went into to see about who might sell good shoes, and I guess I shouldn't have been surprised to find a gay guy there. He directed me to a store way the hell up in Duck called the Dapper Duck, an hour's drive on a two-lane road, and by the time I got back to the house the place was a tiny warzone. None of the breakfast dishes had been put away, even though the house had three times as many people running through it than when I left. I had to squeeze around clusters of Jarem's friends and drinking cousins just to get to the stairs. Mom was back in her caftan, doing her makeup in the bathroom mirror, and I broke the news about the bakery. Buddy, they delivered the cake hours ago, she said, lining her left eye black. Why didn't you call?

Dean was in our room reading something about sales. Where've you been?

Didn't they tell you? I asked.

He went back to his book. He wore swim trunks and a tank. You haven't noticed.

Noticed what?

No one has talked to me, he said. All weekend. Other than you introducing me, no one—not your parents, not your brother—has said even a word to me.

That's not true, I said.

Why would I make it up? he said. I'm not hurt, I'm a big boy, but what's wrong with your family?

I sat down on the bed, crouching so as not to hit my head on the top bunk, and ran a hand up and down his leg. I'm sorry, I said. Let me make it up to you? I ran my hand to his groin and he batted it away.

Why did you invite me here? he asked, putting the book down.

You asked me to! I said.

I asked if I was *going* to be, he said. I was excited to watch you officiate your brother's wedding. It's a side of you I haven't seen before. That's why I wanted to come. And you? What am I here for, exactly?

I didn't know what he wanted to hear to get back to a good mood. He got up and went out to shower and I started getting dressed. Wasn't he here to keep me company, so I didn't have to face my family alone? Or did I just want to show him off, and was he in a bad mood because nobody seemed to care? I was mad, but I wasn't sure who at. Jarem? Moira? With Dean I felt ashamed, which was typical. In the nine months we'd been dating I'd come to see him as the last boy on the dodgeball team, catching every single ball the world threw his way. In not knowing how to be that man I thought I might acquire one, and as I checked my hair in the mirror I saw a glimmer of my brother's face looking back, and I knew that more than anything what I wanted from Dean was for him to make my family proud of me, because I didn't know how to do that alone.

Downstairs, the two missing groomsmen had shown up, but they'd somehow lost Mike, assuming he'd made his way back alone. The good news was that Moira'd found the rings in a pocket of the shorts he'd left behind. Outside she met up with me at the foot of the porch steps and handed me the small velvet pouch.

Best you hold onto these, Reverend.

I asked if she'd called the police yet.

Mike's a bad man sometimes, she said, watching Shelley's niece throw sand at her baby brother. If I called the cops every time this happened, I'd have a pretty shit marriage.

I didn't realize you two had such problems, I said. You've been married just a year.

This made her laugh. We're *fine*. Mike's family's rich and he goes to the gym and does everything I tell him to. This? She shrugged and dumped a handful of sand on the little girl's head. It's just the price I pay to do business.

Shelley's mom made it clear I was not part of the processional, so I went to the beach and stood by the mic before everyone had taken their seats. I couldn't find Dean among all the white chairs. I thought about texting to see where he was, but when I looked there was already a text from him: *Thought it best if I left early. Sorry I had to take the car. Good luck with the ceremony. Let's talk when you get home.* Another casualty of Jarem's big beach wedding. Before I could reply, Dad started up the ukulele music and here were Shelley's bridesmaids in beach-ball orange dresses getting escorted one by one by Jarem's groomsmen in blousy white button-downs and khakis rolled to their calves. They were his bros but I was his brother, and didn't that call for something more? Shelley came last up the aisle with that wide smile of hers, and I thought of Dean and knew what I should do. *Speak from the heart.* It was time for me to say something unrehearsed and honest, but when I tried to feel something for my brother and his bride, when I tried to find words for those feelings, I came up empty. Dad turned the volume down on the music. Everyone looked at me, including strangers up on the decks of all the houses down the coast. It was my turn to talk.

I smiled, I opened the *Illustrated Children's Bible* where I'd tucked my notes, and I read what I'd prepared to.

Welcome, everyone. This gorgeous summer evening, we're here to witness the joining in marriage of Shelley and Jarem, who for those who might not know happens to be my brother. Now, I'm not a priest. That is, not a real one. And I'm not married. That is, not yet—though we'll see what happens in the courts, I guess. My heart was racing. Was I breathing into the mic? Nobody in the crowd moved. Maybe I'm not the best authority on what marriage is, or even love, but I wrote down some thoughts, and I'd like to share them with you all on this happy day. I've always thought of myself as the star of my own movie. I think we all have. It's a way to understand who we are, what our lives mean. Then you grow up. You meet more people. Maybe you get in a relationship. Slowly, you discover that yours isn't the only movie playing. You start to see yourself as a supporting character in someone else's movie, and you think: What does that mean for me? My life, this epic story, is anybody watching it? I guess what I'm saying is that, if anything, marriage is a way out of these kinds of questions. Shelley and Jarem, in coming together, are choosing to no longer star in their own movies. They're starting a new movie together, right at act one. Now they don't have to worry about being bit players. They'll wake every morning and know they're someone else's co-star. I want to say I'm proud of them for taking this step, and I guess I'll also say that Little Brother's jealous that they get to.

Then the rest of the ceremony happened. After Jarem kissed Shelley, they stormed down the aisle together, followed by all of their friends. Everyone in the crowd stood and turned to watch them go, and I was left there on my own.

Another Man's Treasure

WE LIVE IN A PLACE THAT GETS ALL THE TEMPERATURES, 0 to 100. It is not an extreme climate, but it can get there. And when it is extremely cold it is easy to do my job. I can always put on gloves. Some thicker long johns over my thin long johns. But when it is extremely hot I am no good. I cannot collect refuse naked. I cannot remove my skin. In summer, by the end of a shift, when you grab a can of trash and half a bag of refuse spills out of it, the stink of it hits you only right after it hits the ground. And it is a sharp stink, like a doctor's needle stuck right into your throat, and by the time I have gotten all the refuse picked up and tossed into the truck my eyes are burning and tears are adding to all the sweat on my face.

What they say about refuse and secrets is also true. I do not go looking through people's refuse, but I cannot help it if people cannot, or will not, secure their trash bags. I try not to judge and I do not claim to know about people, but in my twelve years in sanitation I have seen skin mags for every taste imaginable, and I have come across torn panties and junk guns and once even a photograph of a grown man with bushy eyebrows lying buck naked on a bed, wearing a pair of ladies' stockings.

One sticky morning in August, behind a house that had been empty for months, I came across the tail of a cat that had been hacked off with a knife, the blood crusted at one end around a nub of bone. It sat on the top of a refuse can as if it had been left there for me. For any animal carcass we were supposed to leave it and call animal control, but I hollered at Randall to kill the motor and come help me look. Neither of us found a body. So I swore and I threw the tail into the back of the truck.

I told Cheryl about it when I got home. I said, It is something sick, Cheryl, what I saw. This is not like hitting a cat with your car on accident, this is some kind of torture.

She was lying on the couch in her sweatpants and one of my old tee shirts that did not fit anymore. Next to the couch I saw a full basket of laundry that was all folded. I could smell the fabric softener, like walking down that aisle of the grocery store. She said, You are so sensitive. Sometimes kids f—— animals up. My brothers put firecrackers all up in frogs all the time and they turned out okay.

Derrick, her older brother, was in his fifties and still dating girls who worked at bars. And not pretty girls, either. And her younger brother, Kevin, took four different kinds of pills every day. I did not say this to Cheryl because she knew it. But I said, Your okay is not my okay. She was watching a talk show, it seemed like. And when I looked to see which one, I saw on the screen a man with black hair like a tire and a beard and a big pregnant belly. I said, Holy h——. And Cheryl said, I know, right? That faggot can get pregnant but not me. And I guess we two wondered together about what kind of world this was now where men can get pregnant. This man was smiling and he had a wife. I did not quite understand it, but it was there on *Oprah* so I did not think it was a hoax.

Cheryl got herself up off the couch and shut off the TV. She said, I am done watching that garbage. Then she went back to the bedroom and I said, Cheryl, you forgot the laundry. And she called out, Bring it in yourself. But I was not about to do her chores for her and besides seconds later she poked her head out. She said, Actually, forget it. You stink and I do not want you stinking up my laundry.

That next Friday, at the same house as last time, I found two squirrel tails laid on the lid of the bin. I shouted at Randall to stop the truck for a bit and found a grocery sack in the other bin and used it to grab the tails to bring back later. I was not about to have to deal with dead animal parts every time I came along to collect this new person's trash. That part of town was where all the Billy-Bobs of our town lived, and on the way over there after my shift ended, I hit potholes bucket deep every other block. The house I needed had bushes all along the front porch that were taller than me. I heard a noise after I knocked on the door and saw in the corner a whole wasps' nest, the bugs buzzing angrily around it. I had to knock a second time before some man opened the door and said, What is it? This guy, he was shorter than me and had a long face like a peanut. He wore a plain white tee shirt tucked into some brown slacks like you might wear to church. I said, My name is Dale Rochester, sir, and I collect refuse on this street. I would like you to take a look in here. Here I opened the bag and tried to show him the squirrel tails. Have you seen these before?

He squinted at me. He said, What is in there? I "ain't" looking in no bag.

Behind the man I heard a voice that said, Who is there?

The man opened the door more to look behind him. I saw a scrawny kid in his underwear. He looked maybe to be in middle school, and you could tell he was the son of the man because he squinted at me the same way. Around the boy, in the room, I saw a big lazy boy recliner and a wooden kitchen chair and a little TV set on a cardboard box. I saw a pizza box on the floor and some live animal traps.

The kid said, What does he want?

The man turned back and looked at me. He looked like he was looking for an answer to his son's question.

I said, Sir, this is the second week in a row that I have found a tail on the top of your trash can. I do not know what it was like where you came from but you cannot put an animal carcass or even parts of animals' bodies with your regular refuse collection.

His son came up and stood right up close by the man's side. He still wore only his jockey shorts, and now he could be seen from the street. If I had a son I never would have let him do this.

The man said, Where we came from people minded their own business.

And I said, What is on or in that refuse can is my business, sir. You have animal parts to get rid of, you call the county. Get animal control down here.

And then the man said something I was not sure I heard right. He said, I am the county.

I did not blink, but I said, I am sorry, sir?

The man crossed his arms and said, Show him, son. And then the son grinned and put his hand inside his father's back pocket. The man just stood there while his son put his hand in. What he pulled out was a policeman's badge and he thrust it up toward my face.

It read Seward County Sheriff's Office. Badge No. 392.

Then the man said, Get the f—— off my property. I told him if he was county he should know the county ordinances. He shut the door on me.

I took the bag of squirrel tails and left it in the bed of his pickup. I figured those tails would be back on the bin the next Friday but I was wrong. I never found animal parts on the trash bin again so I knew it must have been one of them all along.

Then school started and it began to cool down and make all of our lives easier, and the next thing that happened was that I heard from my wife Cheryl's friend about her oldest son. I came home from work one afternoon and I saw Alissa Marie smoking her cigarettes on my patio, complaining to my wife that Aaren, the boy, had had stool thrown at him outside the school.

I said, You know, Alissa Marie, with the way he traipses around town with his clothes cut up it is no surprise the other kids give him a hard time.

Cheryl kicked me in the shin from her patio chair, but I stood firm. Alissa Marie had five kids, two of them boys, and the twelve-year-old had already decided that he was a queer. He told his family over dinner one night. Ever since, he had taken to cutting off the bottom parts of his shirts and most of the legs of his shorts.

I said, It is dangerous. It is an invitation to bullies and perverts. If he were my son I would make him dress normal.

And then Alissa Marie said, Yeah, but he "ain't" your son and last I heard you could not even make a son so I think I will ignore your parenting advice, Dale.

Which meant Cheryl had been sharing our private information again, even after all our fights about it. One time after work, Kenny made a joke about his testicles getting jostled by the ride of our truck, and it was not until they all started cracking up that I realized he was making reference to something I liked for Cheryl to do in the bedroom. Also, she could not be sure it was my fault. We had not seen a doctor yet. But I was not about to get back into this argument in front of company, so instead I just looked at my wife in a way that said we would talk about this later, but she would not meet my eye. She just reached for one of Alissa Marie's Vantages, which she was not supposed to be doing while we were trying to get her pregnant.

This was what it had been like to be married, and there in the shower I wondered how long it could go on. If we did not have a kid, what else were we supposed to do with the rest of our lives? But if we did have a kid what if it was a son? And what if that son said one night that he wanted to be a queer and started dressing himself like Aaren and getting s—— thrown at him at school?

I felt that given the chance Cheryl and I could do a better job raising one kid than the Tschetter-Ziedschlaws had done with their five, so I resolved to call my insurance company about seeing somebody who could get us to make a baby.

The fall came and the Bluejays' new running back had already rushed for 750 yards by the end of September. Cheryl and I went out to a game or two before she lost interest and I had to sit with my old high school buddies. The Watertower Festival happened in October, and though it was mostly an event for people with kids I took Cheryl. We bought a ticket to go up the tower and saw the streets of our town stretch across the prairie. I pointed out our house and Cheryl said, The houses are so small over there, but they were not really that small.

There was also that appointment in Lincoln, where the problem turned out to be with my stuff and not Cheryl's. The doctor was a woman. She made me switch from jockeys to boxers and put me on some pills. Cheryl was very happy it was not her, she said, because to fix that problem would cost a lot more money than to fix me. And I told her that I did not want her sharing this information with anyone, and she said she promised. Then she started fixing me a lot of steaks and burgers for dinner because she thought it would improve my numbers.

One morning Randall overslept, and then we found that no one had filled the truck's tank the previous night. So we were late to our first stop that morning at the middle school. As the truck pulled up near the cafeteria receptacles, there was a cluster of twenty-some-odd kids in our way. I heard Randall hit the horn but the kids were slow in moving, so I hopped off the back to tell them that they were in the way. And then I saw there was a fight going on.

There was a boy on his back on the ground with his legs kicking everywhere. His legs were bare, mostly, and that morning I had to wear a sweatshirt and a hat to say warm. So I knew it had to be Aaren and his short-shorts, and then I saw that his face was hidden under another boy. It was the cop's son again. That boy's legs were also mostly bare, because he had his pants and jockey shorts pulled down past his knees. And he was sitting with his bottom pressed on Aaren's face.

My first thought was: I do not want to have a kid.

My second thought was: Where is a teacher or principal?

The cop's son slammed a fist down on Aaren's belly, and I grabbed him by the neck and tossed him to the ground. Aaren's face was red and wet, and as soon as he was free he scrambled up and began kicking the cop's son in the head. The cop's son could not pull his pants up because he was protecting his head with his arms. I let Aaren get a couple good kicks in, then I grabbed him and held him away at a distance.

Aaren yelled, White trash! Do not ever touch me again!

I told him to stay quiet. I said, Time to walk away.

I let him go and he looked up at me. I pretended for a minute that he was my own son, and I said, Why do you always have to dress like that?

And he said, Why does everyone else get to be the way they want to be but I do not?

The other kids around looked up at me and waited. Even the cop's son did, with his eyes open and not squinting.

I did not have any answer.

Growing up I had always wanted to become what I was supposed to. A high school graduate. A married man. I do not think I was supposed to become a refuse collector, but I think I was supposed to get a job working for the town in one way or another, and I think I was supposed to work outside. I was supposed to be a father by now, and so I was trying.

Which brings me to the next thing that happened. Cheryl and me were in the bedroom because her fertility calendar had said she was making eggs. She was lying in her position as our doctor made her do, the one which helped my seed find hers. And then someone started pounding on the front door. I grabbed my robe and went to answer it and saw the cop standing there with his son.

I stayed polite and asked if I could help him.

He said, I am here to take you into custody. He said, Assault, and abuse of a child.

He was not a big man. He looked like a fresh cadet but his face made him look older. Older than me by almost a decade. I told him what I saw and why I acted the way I did. I made it clear to add that his son had hit Aaren in the stomach. The whole time the kid was shouting, He is lying, Daddy! He is lying! And then I heard Cheryl's voice.

What does this little piglet f——ing want?

Cheryl had always had some kind of hatred for police officers. It was a thing she got from her brothers growing up. It was intense. I tried to explain to her what happened at the middle school, but she was not paying attention. She stood right in the doorway wearing just a tee shirt and her panties. She was making oinking noises, and when I got done explaining she stopped.

She said, This is the little s—— that has been picking on sweet Aaren?

The cop said to me, This your sister? in a way that made his son laugh hard.

I said, Cheryl go back inside the house. Put some clothes on.

She said, I "ain't" going anywhere.

Then she turned to the cop.

She said, You lay one hand on my husband I will f——ing kill your little s—— stain son.

And that is when I got arrested. He was not a big man, but he knew how to take me down. He tugged my arms behind my back and slapped handcuffs on me, and when he set me up I was exposed in my robe. The cop handed the key to his son, who threw it clear over the house. He said, You leave my boy alone, and then they just left, sniggering. It took Cheryl over an hour to find the key.

She wanted to file some kind of charges but I told her it was not worth the trouble. I was not scared, but I did not know my rights in this situation, and then I was mad at myself for not knowing my rights. As a fellow public servant I had always trusted the police, but for the next few days I felt bullied and beat down. I checked in with Mike to fill him in on what went on in case the cop showed up at his house, but he said he knew all about it. He said, Our wives have been on the horn nonstop. I am afraid they got themselves worked into a tizzy. They want to take this to the school board meeting next week.

Mike was in HVAC. He made a lot more money than me, so I did not worry about hurting his feelings when I said, It was just two boys messing around. And you know it would not even be a problem if you and Alissa Marie paid more mind to the way Aaren carried himself around that school.

Mike laughed. He said, Aaren has never skipped school once, did you know that? He gets A's in everything. Even P.E.

I did not know any of that. It was like when people asked me what I did for a living and I would tell them I collected refuse. They would say, Oh, and I could watch their eyes try not to look down at me. I had come to learn that no matter how rich or poor people were, it was hard for them to forget that their household had a servant, and that was the man who took away the refuse. When you collect refuse, you work for everyone. But for me, this was a good thing. I liked to play my part. Little Aaren made himself different from everything everybody knew, and I did not think I would ever understand it.

Cheryl drug me to the school board meeting even though we did not have any schoolchildren. She made me put a tie on. She said, You may be called up to provide testimony.

I told her it was not a trial.

She said, Evidence then. And go run a comb through your hair.

As it turned out, I did not have to say a word. Alissa Marie did all of the talking. She stood right up front of the high school cafeteria and Aaren sat next to her in church clothes. He held his arms across his chest and kept his eyes on the floor. Alissa Marie told the whole room that Aaren was hitting his younger brother now at home. She said, He never did that before the school year started. My sweet boy he has changed and I think we all know why.

The president of the school board interrupted her. He said, It is called having a teenager. Trust me. It is no picnic and I should know.

A lot of people in the room laughed. The president I did not know, but he had a face I kept looking at. A big forehead like a pencil eraser and hairy eyebrows that made his eyes so dark I could not tell their color.

Alissa Marie shook her head. She said, My son is different. I know you all know what I am talking about. It is his cross to bear. But it is unfair that he should have to be attacked for it. If he were a Muslim I am sure you would be listening to me.

Cheryl stood up and said, It is true. You all would.

I grabbed her arm and pulled her back to her seat.

The president said, Misses Cheddar-Seesaw, the school board is not here to give students special treatment. No one else has come forward on this issue. What can we do?

Alissa Marie said, That boy put his bare buttocks on my son. That is sexual harassment. I looked it up. I want him expelled. Aaren is a fighter, but it is not safe for him to come to school now. The other day you know what he asked me? He says to me, "Mom, can you buy me something for school?"

Aaren said, Mom! and tugged at her arm.

But she kept talking: And I says, "Sure, baby, what is it?" And he says, "A gun."

And then the meeting fell apart. Other parents began standing up and shouting that Aaren ought to be expelled. Cheryl stood up with Alissa Marie and shouted at the parents shouting. I watched as Mike put an arm around his boy and led him out the closest exit. The president shouted for everyone to take their seats. He waved his arms in the air, and that is when I realized I had seen him before. Only it was in a picture, wearing just some lady's stockings.

On the drive home, I mentioned it to Cheryl.

She said, Does not surprise me. This f———ed up town is going to s———.

I did not want my wife to be right about our town, but when I thought about it I remembered all the potholes. They used to be filled by Memorial Day and now they just were not filled. The pool my mom used to take me to growing up was now mostly Mexicans, and Randall once said his kid gashed his foot open on some broken glass in the shallow end. Whatever kid Cheryl and I had would not be able to grow up in the town I grew up in, and that hurt me like a punch in the face.

The Tuesday before Thanksgiving we got eight inches of snow and could not drive up to Valentine to see Cheryl's brother Kevin. She and I had our own Thanksgiving, snowed in. It was not nice. It was like the Thanksgiving lunches I remembered from school.

I said, Do they still serve those lunches at school?

She said, How the h——— would I know?

Then she got up and dumped most of the food from her plate in the trash can. In my mind I moved that food from the trash can to our bin out back. From the backyard to the curb. From our curb to the truck. From the truck to the landfill out in Milford. Cheryl never once offered to take out the trash, because the can in the kitchen was where her refuse ended. That was the end of the story, for her.

I was up at five the next morning to get on the truck and pick up half the town's uneaten food. It was the coldest I had felt all year. I forgot a hat and my ears burned all morning. When I got home my walk into the house did not come as a relief like I thought it would. In the living room I saw Cheryl wrapped in blankets, like she had survived a fire. She said, D——— furnace has been out all day. Mike is on his way over.

I said to her, You did not have to call him. I will take a look at it.

She said, Furnaces is his job, honey. He knows what to do, the first time.

I went back to the bedroom to strip and get clean. It was cold enough outside that the food juices had frozen and did not drip on me, but the smell was still there and now in my clothes. And I did not feel that Mike Tschetter-Ziedschlaw was better than me just because he was in HVAC, but all the same I did not want to smell around him when he got here.

There was no hot water, either, but I dealt with it.

I got back to the front of the house and found Mike on the floor outside the utility closet. Cheryl was out in the TV room, not even bothering to watch and learn what Mike was doing. I said, What is the verdict?

He said, Looks like you got a bad gas valve.

I watched him work, ashamed to ask for specifics. It looked like surgery. I said, How have things been with your boy?

Mike sat up on the floor, putting his flashlight back in his tool belt. He said, Not great. He left the house last night after supper and did not come home.

I did not feel like going back out there now that the sun was going down, but I asked if he needed help looking for him.

He said, No, thanks. Alissa Marie has called the police and they say to wait twenty-four hours, which should be any minute now actually. I better get home. He packed up his tool kit and scrambled up off the floor. He said, It will be a few days before I can get a new valve. You got a place to stay?

I said, We can light a fire and live like hobos.

He shook my hand and laughed at my joke. Then he said, I heard about your swimmers, Dale. Do not sweat it. A lot of guys I know have that going on.

I could not say anything in reply. I felt blood rushing to my face as I walked him to the door.

Cheryl was there, her eyes on the TV. She said, He fix it?

And that is when I lost it. I shouted at Cheryl, You are the worst wife a man could have ever found for himself. You do not give a s—— for me.

She said she did not know what I was talking about so I told her what.

I said, I am supposed to be your husband.

She said, You think people care you do not have a lot of sperm?

I said, It makes me feel like I am not even a man. And now everyone else knows it.

Then I grabbed my keys and my coat and I got in my truck and left.

I drove in circles around our town and I made myself be honest with myself. For the first time I thought that not only did I not want to have a kid but I also did not want to have a wife either. How were we supposed to keep living the way we were living? But how could I leave her and find someone else in this small town where all the good girls were married? I did not want to move to some big city and not know who to talk to about getting a job with the sanitation department or who to go to to find a house. And so I was stuck, so I kept driving.

I got fast food and made a plan. I would stop at the places that meant something to me and Cheryl and look for signs. The sun had just sunk. I saw other trucks and cars driving over the packed snow, done with their shopping. Only half of us had our headlights on. I pulled up to the movie theater on Town Square, where we had our first date. It had closed years ago. The marquee that hung over the sidewalk still said THANKS FOR YOUR PATRONAGE, but some kids had chucked rocks at it and almost all the bulbs were shattered. I drove down Fletcher to the Old Crow, where I proposed to Cheryl and got the whole restaurant to applaud when she said yes. It was closed for the holiday weekend. We got married in the Presbyterian church because it had the tallest steeple, and when I drove over there all I saw was a middle-age woman tying her scarf tighter around her neck. And then I was out of places, except for our house, but at that point I could not go back. When was the last time the two of us went out somewhere? I could not think of it at first, but then I thought hard and remembered it was the Watertower Festival, so I drove on out to the interstate.

It was almost dark, but I could still see the water tower get bigger and bigger in silhouette against the sky. I pulled in to the gravel lot at the base of the tower, and when I did I saw the hump of a dead animal on the ground, maybe thirty yards from my headlights. It looked from my seat like a doe had been hit. I opened the door and stepped up to the animal.

And then I saw it was not an animal but a person. It was a boy, his back to me, like he was sleeping. I walked around to look at his face and that is when I knew who it was.

I could not see any blood, but all the same I knew he was dead. I walked back around the body and thought about what to do. I looked closer and saw on the ground, like it was growing out of his rear, a cat's tail.

Then I saw police lights around me. I heard a voice tell me not to move and I expected to see the cop there, and I thought, This is it. I thought I would get some justice. But then a body came around the headlights of the car and I saw it was a woman. I picked up the tail and held it in the air for her to see. I said, I know who killed this boy.

She spoke at me with a very loud voice. What are you doing here?

I said I was just driving around and had found the body. I said, This tail was on the ground right next to him. It is the same thing I saw—

But then she took out her gun and told me to get down on the ground, and before I could explain myself I was in the back of her cruiser being read my rights.

I spent the night in jail, and if I had any relief it was that I had a coat on, because the heat in the cell was broken or turned off as some kind of punishment. I could hear Cheryl's voice somewhere just outside the cell. You f——ing pigs have about two seconds to tell me what the h—— my husband is doing in jail before I call up that Friedman guy on the TV and sic him on all your a—es. Usually I am embarrassed by her when I hear her talk like this, but that morning hearing her voice warmed me up. They told her if she calmed down she could see me and it seemed to work. She showed up outside the cell and I ran to her and took her into my arms. It hurt, the cold bars between us, and I said I was sorry for making her worry.

Cheryl told me what I already knew, which was that they were holding me on charges of tampering with a criminal investigation, and then she told me something I did not know, which was that they were also holding me on suspicion of murder. She said, Which is crazy because it is a suicide. He jumped, the poor boy.

And I said, He did not jump. He was thrown off that water tower and I know who did it, but no one will listen.

Cheryl said I had to shut up or they would use my words against me. So I shut up. I shut up for the rest of the day I was in that jail cell. I shut up when they asked me about the tail. I shut up when they asked me about the fight Aaren had got in. I shut up even when they asked me if I wanted something to eat, and then right as the light outside was starting to fade they came to the cell and told me I could go.

I said, Go where?

They said, Go home. You are off the hook.

It left me confused, but they said the details were confidential. It was still under investigation. At home that night, snuggled like an Eskimo under every blanket we owned, my chest felt tight and hot, and I wished I had done everything different. Running out on my wife. Breaking up that fight. The tails. I wished I had been smarter and known how to bring about some justice. I needed help and I wanted to tell Cheryl about my suspicions, but she would have told the Tschetter-Ziedschlaws, and how could I come up with an answer for them when they asked me why of all the things to leave frozen on the ground I had chosen their dead son?

After work the next day I drove to the cop's house and peeked through the windows. Nobody answered the door when I knocked and there was no truck in the driveway. It took me a long time on the phone with the police to get them to give me his name, and when they did they said, Officer Steis. He had resigned a week ago. He left no forwarding address. I told them that that seemed suspicious. I said, I do not know how to do your job but I would give him a phone call. The investigating officer did not like to hear this. Cheryl did not either. She said, You keep stirring up trouble when all Mike and Alissa Marie want is to lay their son to rest.

That boy killed Aaren, I said. I know it.

But here is the thing: I did not know it. I could not prove that the tail had been cut off by Officer Steis or his son. I only had a suspicion, and was it not true that suspicions turned the people in your life into suspects?

On Wednesday I took a day off and Cheryl and I went to the funeral. Together we walked up to the casket to look at Aaren there.

Cheryl was crying. His face had more color on it than when I had last seen it, and he had a different expression, too. He seemed to be lost, as though he did not understand what had happened to him. And I did not understand it either. Throughout the service I rolled the program into a tight coil. It did not matter what I thought I knew, because a murder was not more sad than a suicide. It was not less sad, either. It was just sad. It was sad that Aaren was gone, and that it was forever. It was a sad world that made Mike and Alissa Marie live the rest of their lives with that hole his death had made, a world it would be hard to ever raise a child in. I sat very still in my pew and tried to picture that hole. I felt in my mind that if I ever found myself down there, it would be very dark and very cold, and the fact that everyone else in my little town was standing with me would make the place no less lonely, and no less horrible.

Irgendwo, Nirgendwo

THEY SIT LIKE LUMPS AT THE KITCHEN TABLE COVERED by a worn and greying cloth, milkdregs ghosting the glass of two tumblers. Their four feet dangle inches above the floor as Opa sucks his horehound. They can hear it slopping around, see it burrowing there behind his potato jowls. They smell the burnt-tire funk of it.

It's July and the brothers are long enough out of school that their stretched and empty afternoons have become *kind of boring,* they say. Nowadays, the two are *mostly bored.* Opa's fat hand claps the table. He tongues his candy to the far end of the mouth and cries, Nonsense. There is no mostly, he tells them. No kind of. Either you are bored or you are not, and if you are it is only you who is to blame. From the other room come the strangled words of their mother shouting at her mother. Opa nudges the boys out to the front porch. There he lowers his flanks onto a pine rocker.

["Actually," said Kurt, sipping the beer she'd bought, "it was a lot like the one your aunt left behind. You know the one I mean?"]

There's an *oomph* and a curse and the old man begins to teach the boys a game. He calls it a game of discipline and discovery. To play, the boys must only step outside their front door and watch and listen and remember. If a dog is barking, turn right, and continue until either he has stopped barking or you no longer can hear him. If you hear a car horn, turn left. If you hear a car door slam, turn around. Cross the street if someone within your range of vision wears a purple shirt. "Write ziss down!" Opa implores the boys in the accent they still find funny. Kurt runs inside for a strip of paper hung by the telephone. His mother is at the bottom of the stairs, accepting from her mother a slip of crisp green bills. She tells him it's time to leave. Kurt runs back to the porch, and Opa plucks one of the felt-tip pens he keeps in his shirt pocket. He writes all his rules down, and after covering both recto and verso in blooming black ink the brothers are given the list.

It will fill their empty days well into adulthood.

"What do we call it?" Thomas asks Opa.

Opa pauses three or four seconds and gives a little shrug.

"Irgendwo, Nirgendwo."

["I always assumed he'd made the whole thing up," Kurt said. "I always thought it was something silly."]

He bites the horehound in two and the brothers feel their own teeth crumbling. Their mother is out by the car with her keys. Opa walks wordlessly inside and they don't see him again for another two years, when at his funeral they learn his Christian name.

"It's Kurt," says Thomas.

Many years later they lived together in a three-bedroom prairie-style house at the intersection of Madison and Schultz. There was a gabled roof, and a flagstone porch stretched across the front like a rampart. Kurt was younger and got to fill the extra bedroom with his carvings, for he'd done the finding and buying of the house, back on the eve of his master's defense. Thomas had moved in after his legs both broke—this from the fainting of his ladder-holding and heat-exhausted former business partner—and his walkup became unwalkuptoable. They shared chores happily. Kurt cut the lawn and pruned the elms and bought each spring some plants to set into the hard clay. Snapdragons. Dusty miller. Wax begonias. The work would take hours, and then Thomas would bring out iced tea and sandwiches, and the brothers would outpost to the intersection's opposite corner to better admire the yard's new texture. "Women like a man who's handy around the house," Kurt often said, and Thomas would agree and add that they also liked a man who was handy around the kitchen.

"That's what I said," said Kurt. "The kitchen is part of the house."

It was, in full, Thomas's part of the house, where he kept his skillets and herbs and at mealtimes favored the hearty meats and starches of German cuisine as passed down to him from their Oma: *knödeln, würstchen, sauerbraten, spätzle.* He worked in an outdoor mall along the city's main artery, at a store that sold implements and furnishings for the kitchen. He spent his shifts womanizing and stocking shelves in priggish cogitation. How did his ancestors ever manage *Wiener schnitzel* without a tenderizer springloaded with forty-eight strategically placed stainless-steel blades? What had driven the customers he liked to smile at to no longer smile back? He wasn't even fifty.

And he wasn't fifty but he was getting close. Kurt, at forty-four, was a senior engineer in a downtown recording studio that specialized in voiceover work. This had, by design, little bearing on the life of a man with enthusiasms. Kurt was a nosepicker. Paradise for him was a sharp blade and a well-lamped room full of unadulterated oak. After fourteen years of shared space, if strife came between the brothers it came whenever one confused sharing with annexing—as Thomas had one summer afternoon after a wet and eventless morning shift. From the foyer he called his brother's name and on no response mounted the stairs and knocked twice on his workroom's door before opening it. "You busy?" he asked. "I'm restless."

"You could have yourself a nap," Kurt suggested from behind magnifying goggles.

"What you got there?" he asked, leaning in further.

"Lovespoon," Kurt said. "In sycamore."

It looked to Thomas like a tongue depressor. Another piece of shelfmeat. Outside, the rain had stopped, so Thomas knew what to do. He clapped twice and said, "Out the door, brother." It had become their one modification to Opa's famous game, this formal gesture toward commencing play. Thomas had come up with it, as well as its corollary that—provided no game had been played the previous two days—a brother could not refuse the request. Kurt took a deep breath and set his work in a satin-lined box.

"We can't keep playing this game forever," he said.

After just four blocks of wanderings, Kurt pulled ahead in the contest over who could heed cues first, a thing Thomas tallied alone, shuffling along behind his brother, slowed by leg pain and focusing more on the sidewalk than the world's shifting daylight. He tried in his mind to settle some confusing thoughts on animals. Did boy kangaroos have pockets or just girl kangaroos? Did insects die every winter, or just sleep through it? Kurt called out, "Flat tire. Left," and sure enough there it was on an old conversion van parked on the grass of a defunct daycare. Thomas dropped his gaze back to the ground, Kurt's feet well beyond the edge of his sightline, and he turned left when he saw the sidewalk open in that direction. He walked a few paces before he heard Kurt call out his name.

He looked up. Kurt hadn't turned and was standing halfway to the block's next corner. Thomas, however, was now facing a house, with a high black gambrel jutting up from a battlefront of overgrown cypresses. It was a place he'd never irgendwo'd to before. On its top floor were two windows backed with thick, dusty drapes, shutting the house off to the world like the eyes of a blind man. Thomas took a few steps forward. Behind the trees was a porch with a rocking chair. It looked hand-carved.

"Come look at this, brother," he said.

"Let's keep going," Kurt said. "We go in your direction and the game will be over."

"Not necessarily."

Thomas walked up to the porch and in a short time Kurt was running a finger along the rocker's rough curve. "Pine," he said. "A poor finishing job, that's for certain."

He gave the thing a sad push, and Thomas noticed bells clanging in the distance. Was it four o'clock? "Church bells," he said. "Turn right."

He indicated the house's front door.

Kurt looked up. "My right takes us back to the street, Thomas."

"Not mine," he said. "And I noticed the cue."

No doorbell button hung anywhere near the entrance, so Thomas knocked four times on the door's four-paned window. His brother stooped and peered through the gauzy cloth that hung behind the glass. They heard nothing. Thomas tried the doorknob. "Thomas!" Kurt said, grabbing at his hand, but the knob turned and the door opened and a chill crept out from around the jamb.

Now they were trespassing in earnest.

They heard a voice from deep inside the house. "Hello? Ally?"

Thomas stepped into the foyer. "Hello, there!"

A wide wooden staircase bowed to the left and up to the home's second floor. At the landing stood a person in a wide white dress, but the house was filled with enough shadows that it was hard to make out a face. Thomas could see a bright flame of red hair.

"I own two guns," the voice said. "That's one for each of your corpses if you take another step in my home."

Thomas raised his hands like at a stickup, and she began descending, stair by stair.

"Ma'am," said Thomas, "we're sorry to bother you, but my brother and I were playing a game and it led us here. To your house here." Kurt stood behind him in the doorway. The light from the door made a slanted box on the patterned rug. It lit the woman up when she got to the final step, where she stopped as though to remain out of reach. She bore no arms or firepower.

"Oh, my," she said, peering into Thomas's face. "You've been playing Irgendwo, Nirgendwo, haven't you?" She hit the words with the swallowed *R*'s and vowels of pristine *Hochdeutsch.* From another person's lips their game sounded like a curse.

"You know it?" Thomas asked.

"Is that cherry?" Kurt asked. Thomas and the woman followed Kurt's pointing finger to the acorn that topped the stairs' newelpost.

The woman turned and touched it, as though checking its heat. "I guess you know what you're talking about," she said. In the dress, her full arms were bare and pale. Thomas imagined they'd feel like a warm coat wrapped around him.

She looked at Kurt. "What's your name?"

"Kurt," said Kurt. "This is my brother, Thomas."

"You can come get a closer look if you want." She then stepped further into the foyer, as though to give Kurt room for inspection. He stepped in past the length of the rug and began rapping on the ornament.

"Cherry," he said. "Nice work."

"It's amazing," Thomas said. "I didn't think anyone else knew about our game." He watched the loose muscles swell in the woman's back as she began to smooth the bust of her dress.

"I'm sorry for all that about guns earlier," she said. "But all the same I need to ask you both to leave."

Kurt's hand slowly dropped from the acorn, and as it did his eyes seemed to follow the line of the banister all the way to the top of the house. He stood there, jaw slack. There was wood around every door, Thomas could tell. Every wall molded with it.

"It's beautiful in here," Kurt said. The woman in white moved closer to him, and from where Thomas stood, her shadow cast by the open doorway's light slid like a serpent up the stairs. Her glowing body moved between them, eclipsing his brother from view.

"Gentlemen, please," she said, and they obeyed and left the house.

It had always been only theirs. For years Thomas had felt that Opa had shared with him and Kurt some kind of heirloom, the list of cues a recipe that generations of Opas must have cached in a series of heavy Bibles. By his teens he wised up. He read the list for what it was: an off-the-cuff mess to keep listless kids busy. Still, it had been their mess, the brothers', and of the two of them it was Thomas who worked the hardest over the years at its preservation. *It's our tradition,* he'd insist. *Our family's tradition.* Now, suddenly, it was also somebody else's. Perhaps the game wasn't such a rare thing. Perhaps it was as public as a lynching. Thomas told Kurt at the supermarket a few days later that they owed it to their mother to find out.

"What's Ma got to do with anything?" Kurt said. He stopped the cart at the meats case.

Thomas scanned the shelves for veal. "You never gave her enough credit," he said.

"She was a drunk, Thomas."

"I'm not having this argument with you again," he said. He dropped a pack of four thick cutlets into the cart. "My point is that we need to talk to that woman. And I would have been able to the other day if you hadn't gone ape over that dumb acorn."

Kurt took the veal out of the cart and set it back in the cooler. "You know what they do to those calves," he said.

"I want to invite her to dinner," said Thomas. "She probably likes a good schnitzel."

"Make it with pork, then," Kurt said. "It's less than half the price."

They must have been a sight, two grown men bickering like old marrieds. It was clear from the twin gauntness of their faces that they were brothers, but despite Kurt's pipsqueak frame his loafers and plaid shirt buttoned to the chin made him seem the elder. Around them, hausfraus put some muscle behind their brimming carts as they bent around the aisles, not one of them paying these men any mind. Thomas fell instantly in love with each.

"Are you telling me you don't want to treat her right?" he asked his brother. Kurt sighed and brought the veal back out of the case.

"Don't forget your scrip," he reminded Thomas.

And though he'd planned it all so carefully the dinner, two nights later, was a disaster. Lynne, for that was her spinstery name, had insisted on bringing her niece along. Ally was a twig-thin veterinarian, and she sat to his right, opposite Lynne, piercing each pea separately with the same fork tine in a distracting way that made Thomas sweat and gulp at his Riesling. On the question of Irgendwo, Nirgendwo, Lynne mentioned only that her greataunt had taught her the game, but whether this aunt was related to or even knew their Opa was lost to family histories. That each relative grew up on opposite sides of the Iron Curtain made any connection unlikely, so Thomas—noting the way Lynne held Ally's hand in her own on their arrival—saw in the niece a possibility for connection. "So, Ally, can I ask?" he asked. "How did you lose your parents?"

His own father had walked out on his infant children, and Mom died too young. The pain of this was all he'd meant to share.

"That's such a horrible thing to presume," Lynne said, looking at Thomas for the first time that night. "Nothing, that's your answer."

"They run an amusement park back east," Ally said. She had tiny teeth, like an animal.

"Well, I guess I'm sorry," Thomas said.

A stretch of silence. Ally finished with the peas and laid her fork next to her plate so slowly it didn't make a noise. She stayed focused on her lap. Lynne had arrived with the wine bottle in a brown paper bag and her red hair down past her shoulders, and Thomas watched this hair catch and glimmer the lamplight like the darting flames of a campfire. She sat with her head propped wearily on one hand, elbow inelegantly dug into on the table. Everyone ate as quickly as etiquette allowed. Kurt added nothing to the conversation but this: "More wine, Miss Lynne?"

Here Lynne seemed to unfold herself and beam. She accepted more wine, and Kurt poured another few inches in her glass. He smiled, charitably, and went back to his plate. "You don't say much," Lynne said. Her fingers were strumming the strands of her hair like a harp. "I like people who don't say much. I consider it a sign of intelligence."

This wine tasted cheap, Thomas decided.

"And I like people who are good with their hands," she said. "Look, Ally. Look at his hands. Have you ever seen such good hands? Wouldn't it be nice to have a man like that around the house?"

Kurt laughed at this and offered his right hand for inspection, and for Thomas that was the end of the dinner.

They were to be married, but another year passed through two wet seasons before either Lynne or Kurt saw this to be true, their evenings together, just once or twice a week, spent touring galleries or sitting bisected by popcorn bowls on her rumpus-room sofa, following their favorite serial costume dramas. They were inside people. They went Dutch on dinners. It wasn't a passionless courtship—Kurt's first night spent at Lynne's involved his muting with wet kisses the screams his fingers were working out of her—but at her age it was no good swooning around town like teenaged horndogs. And Kurt agreed: there was little sense in delay. Maybe it was too soon. Alone in her Spartan office, between counseling sessions with anorexic runaways and the recidivistically truant, Lynne wondered whether she weren't settling for the first man to walk stably into her life. Kurt was young, for her. He liked junky foods, and he did a much less clandestine job of fingercleaning his nose than Lynne imagined he thought he did. She liked that he was busy enough with his own life that fitting hers—itself no idle week at the beach—alongside it came with logistical challenges. When he got down on a knee on her front porch in their ninth month together she saw at last in him a kind of clarity, and a voice somewhere inside her announced: This is it. You get someone to share this life with, or you take it all on yourself.

She chose sharing.

It became another logistical puzzle. Who'd move in with whom? She'd raised the question one cold morning over poached eggs—her breakfast for the last forty-three years—and he said, "You'll move in here, of course," as though that were the end of the conversation. She tugged her robe more shut and slid deeper into the corner of the banquette. Hadn't he found her house so beautiful? Maybe it *was* too dark for newlyweds, and even if she took down the blackout drapes her mother had installed after her father'd been pink-slipped and went chronically insomniacal, it was as though every window in the house faced a wall of sunless brick. And there was, yes, that mold problem in the basement. The poor water pressure that kept Kurt rinsing his greying mane much longer than he could stand to. But this was her family's home, she reminded him. Kurt's house had been little more than a market steal.

"I know that," he said. "That's why I think you should sell it to Ally. Keep it in the family."

Kurt and his sequestered decisions! She took the porcelain creamer and filled her half-empty teacup to the brim. Then she stood without a word and headed upstairs to get dressed, leaving the over-creamed tea to clot and get cold. Was she being a child? In time she came to imagine the weekends with her niece, hanging wallpaper together to make the place a home for her and whatever family she may find for herself one day. The question now was who would tell Thomas. Kurt offered to sit down with him, but Lynne wouldn't allow it. "He's already furious with me," she said. Throughout their steady courtship Thomas became a ghost when Lynne was in the house, making himself heard but never seen. Kurt said he'd been taking on more overtime, and Lynne took it as a form of surrender.

Through an in-store ambush during one of these overtime shifts, Lynne got him to agree to meet her at Unny's one frigid Saturday in late April. Kurt had mentioned it as his brother's favorite bar. It was dark, which Lynne liked, but she found its amateurish acrylics of Hollywood starlets and its wall of pickle-card machines as dismaying as its name. Who was this a bar for? Thomas showed up late, face pinkly windblown and sniffling. He held up a finger and the blonde bartender in a man's ribbed undershirt slid a bottle across to him. Thomas brought the bottle to Lynne's distant table and sat down with his coat still on.

"I just want to say two things," he said. Then he drank thirstily from the bottle. "First, I am very happy for you and my brother. Second, I'm upset that you've never cared to get to know me."

He took a deep breath and then another long pull.

"There," he said, satisfied.

It was four thirty in the afternoon. Lynne had paid for a Diet Sprite, but what she had been given was a Sprite.

"That's not true, Thomas," she said.

"It is," he said. "But I'm over it. Like I said, I'm happy for you guys."

Once, early in her career, she'd been assigned a ten-year-old who'd been picked up by the cops while beating his six-year-old sister with a hammer. Robbie was his name. Robbie had the habit of negating everything she said. No he did not do a bad thing. Yes he did too have lots of friends. It took her a week of work to remember that open-ended questions were harder to say no to.

"Why do you think I don't care to know you?" she asked Thomas.

She waited patiently for him to respond.

"*I* invited you to dinner," he said. "Not Kurt."

"What?"

"I'm not talking about who you fell for. I'm not jealous. But since I invited you, the least you could do was talk to me. I just wanted to know about the game. Was that such a terrible topic of conversation?"

In this dim light he looked like a kind of troll, dark and wrinkled. She wanted one thing from him, to cross this bridge just once and thus forever, and she saw in this sick bar that the story of her dalliance with Irgendwo, Nirgendwo was the price she'd need to pay.

"Go order me a whiskey and water," she said, "and I'll tell you everything you want to know."

Tante Beate is what she calls her. *Tante Beate oughta taunt a bee.* Her brother is too young to call her anything. Lynne is nine. It begins on a hot afternoon. Tante Beate has spent each of the last two days of their visit on her porch, in her rocking chair, swatting flies and grabbing periodically at a sweat-beaded beer glass on the wrought-iron side table. Lynne has sat with jacks by the steps, watching. On this day, day three, Tante Beate has a question for Lynne: What does Lynne want to be when she is grown up? Lynne, a good girl, says a doctor or a lawyer. "*Ja, gut,*" Tante Beate says. She rocks in a long skirt and stockings. Sensible shoes and white V-necked T-shirt. And what does Lynne want to *have* when she is grown up? Lynne, in her yellow jumper, does not have an answer. Tante Beate slaps at a fly and stops for a moment her rocking.

"But you must think of this now," she says. Her eyes behind her eyeglasses are enormous. "Me, I have nothing."

She speaks so slowly.

"And so I am nothing."

Lynne's jacks ball bounces off the porch and is lost to some holly.

"*Komm,*" Tante Beate says, eyeing her wristwatch. The woman leads Lynne to the passenger seat of her truck, and they drive off on her weekly round of schnapps deliveries. In the truck she begins to teach Lynne a game. "You cannot know when you will ever find something," she says. "If you find it it has been hidden, and if you knew where it was hidden you could go and you could take it, yes? A husband. A career. A nice house to live in. If you go out and seek these things they will hide from you. You will need to sneak up on them. Now *pass auf.*"

["That was my introduction," Lynne said, spinning her whiskey glass in one hand. Thomas started to remove his coat. "I never wrote it all down, but I never had to."]

It is near dinnertime when Tante Beate is done with her deliveries, but before she heads back to her farmhouse she drives Lynne to the county fair. They have time only to visit the animals in the petting zoo. The fair redundantly has farm animals to pet. Some sheep and goats and a tiny pony small enough for Lynne to ride. They also have a baby kangaroo and they have a tortoise as big as a tire. Then Lynne comes near the far end of the zoo, and there behind a low fence stand two zebras and an ostrich. She keeps her distance from the bird; its neck is alarming and its head is very quick. Lynne asks Tante Beate how many stripes the zebras have. She looks down at her grandniece scornfully and says everyone knows they have only two, and she points. "This one and the other one."

["I never had any pets," Lynne said. Thomas didn't understand. "I didn't want children. I'd decided by then I wanted just to know things, not be with them."]

She sleeps that night like a cold, running river and rises early the next morning. After her juice and scrambled eggs she sneaks a handful of dates into the pocket of her jumper and leaves through the back door. Here, she cocks her ear away from the road to catch the windgusts and birdsong Tante Beate told her to listen for. She is off in seconds when a passing truck blows its horn to signal hello to her porchsitting parents. Soon she is wandering, snaking random box patterns through the fields. She doesn't think about whether anyone is watching her. She plays the game she's taught and waits to find what she needs to have.

In time she's walked through the line of trees that seems miles from Tante's house. She has never been this far before on foot, and the game leads her deeper into the forest. Here is a different terrain to pass through. A creek; she hops onto a rock to cross it. Sticks crunch underfoot. She is nearly out of dates when a new sound hits her ear. Low. Angry. A man? The sound comes from the distant right, but the sound dictates that she must head to the left. It comes again. Was it *Help?* Lynne is stuck between decisions. The noise comes once more, quieter this time, and she breaks the rules. She goes right. Though she can feel she is getting closer, the noise is getting softer. Up a hill the trees thin out, and the forest air gets brighter and warmer. The sun is high by now and shines through the trees and lights up the forest floor, and in this way she's able to see him clearly, as though spotlit on a stage. It's a man on the ground. He is older than her father but younger than Tante Beate. He has the trunk of a tree lying across his body, just a few feet from a ripped stump. The tree's trunk is almost as thick as the man's. Lynne steps closer. She stands over him. He has a string of blood hanging out the side of his mouth. His breaths are shallow, and he sweats. There's an axe inches from his open hand.

He tries to say something but doesn't have the air.

Lynne panics. She tries to lift the trunk but cannot make it move. The man groans at her attempt. She starts to cry. "I don't know what to do," she says.

["Playing in the country is different from playing in the city," Lynne told Thomas, holding his eyes with her eyes. "You go for much longer stretches. You find yourself very far from home. You can't know what it's like until you do it." Thomas didn't say anything.]

The man looks right into her. He has a close grey beard and a red bandana on his head. She looks at him and watches as he takes one quick breath. Then he takes another. His eyes stay open when he stops breathing, and she sees him die and lay still.

["The game led me there," Lynne said. "That's what it thought I was supposed to find."]

She is afraid to leave the body alone, so she sits and cries, choking and sobbing. She places a date in the dead man's palm.

["Your aunt was wrong," Thomas said. "Don't you see? It brought Kurt to you. You didn't have to go looking."]

It's hours before anyone comes looking for her. Back at Tante's her mother holds her in her lap and pets her hair and says "Hush" while her aunt sips yet another beer. She never plays Irgendwo, Nirgendwo again. She tries to shake its rules from the tight vines of her memory, but she fails.

Another year passed like a stomachache. Lynne and Kurt married at the Lutheran church on N Street, the one with all the stained glass. Lynne moved out of her house just nominally, leaving behind whatever Kurt already had one of. Her bed. Her dining table. The components to errant kitchen gadgets. On the day of the move, Ally stood in rooms full of stuff and pointed for the men in coveralls at the empty spots where her ten pieces of furniture might fit. Every day she woke up in and came home to this cramped house, living her life in what felt like a mausoleum to her father's side of the family.

At work she'd become a hag. "He's eighteen years old," she said one morning to the owner of an English pointer who was on her fourth teary tissue. Outside the clinic, there was a foot of snow on the ground, and the wind blew so hard she could hear it whistle. "I mean you're free to set him up for dialysis three times a week. I can do that for you if you want. But in this economy?"

People held on for too long. Convincing pet owners of this was harder work than actually performing their desired surgeries. Why couldn't Ally just take their money?

That afternoon a report came over the radio of another storm front, an additional six to eight inches pending. Ally had her office administrator cancel the rest of her appointments, and driving home she felt rebellious and alive. She was back at the house before three. Her answering machine had its light blinking. It was Thomas, asking her out. Asking her out over her answering machine: "Not a date, ha ha, but just grab coffee sometime?" She hadn't seen him since the wedding, and where had he got her number from? Her mood worsened. Outside, the sky was merely overcast, but here in her front hall it felt like nighttime. Any light that could come to the front of the house was blocked by the frontyard's wall of cypresses, which last fall had developed a virus—"Cypress canker," the tree man had diagnosed—and would have to be torn out this spring. Another thing to pay for, like the dedicated showerhead she put in the master bathroom, the bug screens in the windows, water in the fridge door. She liked old houses—the wood! the surplus rooms!—but with this one she felt suckered. No matter how much plastic she blowdried taut across the windows, she moved from room to room as though through a walk-in freezer. Blessed by a working fireplace—she had to pay for chimney sweeping—she'd ordered a whole cord of wood online, but getting it to catch and hold a fire took an entire Sunday edition. "Too green," Kurt had pronounced one night the newlyweds were over for dinner. "You should get some real kindling." Ally bought an electric heater instead, one she could wheel to whatever room she had to stand in. Her gas and electric bills for the month of January totaled five hundred eighty dollars.

The weathermen were wrong. That evening just two more inches had dropped, and then to Ally's relief a warm front moved through the following week, melting the snow from the sidewalks and much of her front lawn. She wasted no time in convincing Aunt Lynne to come pick up more of her furniture, namely the bookshelves that lined a wall in an upstairs room which Ally wanted to line with aquariums—for what kind of veterinarian didn't have any pets? It was blistering but sunny that Saturday, and Lynne drove up in her station wagon around 4:30, stepping out with enormous sunglasses and a set of white earmuffs smacked like snowballs against her skull. "I don't know how I'm going to make any room," she said, embracing her niece on the porch. She smelled of warm wet dough. "Kurt tells me just to sell everything, but. . . ."

"What about this rocking chair?" Ally said. "I think it'll fit."

"This old thing?" Lynne gave it a little push. "I don't know. Kurt doesn't want to clutter the porch with two chairs."

"But there are two of you."

"Well," she said, and moved to open the door. "So brisk today! Honey, do you have any coffee?"

Marriage had taken away her aunt and replaced her with this sunny ski bunny. Or was it the house that'd done it? Lynne looked, in those days, as though she'd been liberated from some cold prison. All the more reason to get her stuff out of there, exorcise those demons. As they headed back to the kitchen she could see the breezy, vacant smile on her aunt's face as she cataloged the alterations Ally had made since her last visit. "It's lovely to see you make my house your own," she said, running a finger along the old Formica table Ally'd picked up at a junk store the previous week. This was emblematic. For spinster Lynne, very little had been lovely. Companionship had been grossly overrated, but now here was her aunt asking whether she had anybody else in her life.

Ally pulled a couple of mugs from the cabinet. "Actually, Thomas called me," she said.

"Kurt's Thomas?"

"He said he wanted to take me out sometime."

Lynne pulled open a drawer full of tea towels. "He's too old for you," she said, rummaging.

"Here," Ally said, taking a spoon from her utensil drawer and sliding over the sugar bowl. "I thought you drank tea."

Lynne shrugged. "I wonder what his angle is."

"His angle?"

"Are you going to call him back?" she asked.

Was Ally going to call him back? Thomas was too old for her, and he was a fool. But she remembered his cooking and thought if anything she'd get a warm meal out of it. A warm house.

Upstairs, the chill was somehow worse for Lynne and she asked to borrow a sweater. Then they stood facing the bookshelves like a rival tag team. They were cheap pieces, bought in a box at a big-box store, made of particleboard and hex-keyed together within minutes. She instructed Lynne to stand and hold the top left corner while Ally would stoop and lift from the bottom right. "It's the best way to go down stairs," she said. And on three Ally stood and lifted the bookshelf. The thing wasn't more than five feet tall, but something in her trajectory threw Lynne off, and her aunt dropped her end on the floor, cracking one of the boards in half.

"Ally! My shelf!"

Ally set her end on the ground. "I'm sorry, I thought you had it."

Lynne just stood there staring. "It's all junk anyway. Just throw it out," she said. "Or donate it to the homeless." She left with nothing in her wagon except Ally's sweater.

In time, she decided to give Thomas a call. She felt she was getting frigid. Thomas with his Lotharial delusions made her sad, but he was also a man to talk to. On the phone, he spoke at a clip and insisted on picking her up at the house, and before she could refuse he named a day and time and hung up the phone.

He was ten minutes late, and he looked terrible. It was another bright day with another fresh batch of snow on the ground, but even with all the excess sun bouncing everywhere Thomas's face was dark and deathly, mudpuddles under his sourmilk eyes. It was like seeing an abused animal gaze wetly out from her TV screen.

"Sorry I'm late," he said. His breath had the sharp, burnt smell of a lifelong smoker. "I don't have an excuse. Should we take a little walk?"

It was twenty-eight degrees out, but here was a form of desperation she hadn't expected. She stood in her vestibule, letting even more cold air fill her house. How had this change in him happened?

"I know it's cold," he said. "I brought a thermos."

And so he had. She locked the front door behind her, and he filled its cap—tepid but strong. He walked and she followed, turning wherever he turned. He had a cripple's amble, she noticed, cadenced like a motor that wouldn't turn over.

"So how is your new place?" she asked.

He was crashing on the couch of a co-worker, he explained. For the time being. Across the street a woman with bulging plastic sacks hanging from both fists hip-slammed her car's door shut. Thomas stopped in place and led Ally back the way they'd come. Her hackles flared up. These were the wanderings of a crazy person.

"It's actually why I wanted to see you," he said. "You got that whole house to yourself. Maybe you could use some help?"

Was it a marriage proposal, Thomas trying desperately to follow in his brother's recent rite of passage? Moving out of that house must have killed him, or a part of him. She asked whether he'd been spending any time over there since the wedding.

"They had me over weeks ago for some dry lamb stew," he said. "I've got an open invitation, but I've been busy, you know?"

She finished the last of her little lid of coffee and passed it back. By now they were moving toward a neighborhood she liked not to move toward. "Where are we headed?" she asked.

"Oh, anywhere," he said. "And nowhere."

"This is that game you and Kurt play."

Thomas nodded. "Used to."

"You just wander around town, is that it?"

He laughed and began explaining the rules. The whole thing sounded tragic to Ally. The helplessness of it. Removing yourself from a safe known place and letting the world throw you somewhere scary and lost—who'd make a game out of it?

"And you're still playing it," she said. "All grown up."

"Well, it kept us together," he said.

Who'd ever teach it to antsy children?

"And where has it got you?" Ally asked.

Thomas stopped, held a hand to the small of his back. "Right here," he said. "I'm right here, and I'm looking at you."

It was a short date, if it was a date. On the walk home, they crossed the street at the high school, and just at the curb Thomas fell sideways into Ally. She caught him and held him steady as he regained his footing. "Sorry," he said. "Doc says I ought to get a cane."

"You know," she said. "I'm really happy living on my own."

She looked up at him and saw that he was smiling. "I figured you'd say that," he said. "You've always been a loner."

It could have been the sourness of the coffee, but hearing this from a virtual stranger was like bile on the tongue. Around them the wind picked up, and the bare branches of the trees that lined this street shimmied like skeletons. Was it true? She had a response cooking, but here they were: back at her lonely home.

"Tomorrow's my birthday," Thomas announced at her porch. "I'll be fifty, can you believe it?"

She tried to smile. "We should all get dinner."

"One half of one whole century."

"Another half to go," she said. "I'm sure."

Thomas dug something out of his coat pocket. "I got you this," he said, handing it over. It was a little spoon made from wood, with a handle like a mess of serpents knotted together. "It's a lovespoon," he said. "It doesn't mean anything."

"It's nice," she said. She had to get inside.

"Happy housewarming," Thomas said. She watched him amble down her walkway, and shut herself back in her house. Coming out of the gloom of his sad game she felt responsible, somehow. Wasn't this the problem with marriages—they got you involved in people you needn't be involved with? Who was Thomas other than her father's sister's husband's brother? Who was he to be asking so much of her? Ally stood in her foyer for a long time, rubbing her thumb over the spoon's bowl as if for warmth. She decided Thomas was wrong. She didn't want to be alone, but more than money or the love of another person she wanted to move to a city where everyone was a stranger. Including herself. Especially herself.

Ally tried to make a dinner of roasted root vegetables but felt so cold in the kitchen as the sun began to set that her frozen, shivery fingers didn't work. Instead, she heated a can of soup on the stove and carried it with both hands into the living room, kicking the power button on the heater parked inches from her easychair. Its power light stayed dark. She set the soup down on the end table, turned the power off and back on. Still nothing. She checked the cord, the outlet. Like a bum leg, it had gone out on her. She fell down into the chair, her life this deserted corridor. It would be another night of this. Another year. She wasn't cold, is what she told herself. She had only been made cold.

Ally looked over at the fireplace, where logs had been sitting, decoratively, in her hearth all winter. *Too green.* A good fire needed kindling, and as she ate her soup she surveyed the wood in the house. Lynne's bookcases weren't real, and she wasn't ready to burn Thomas's frightful lovespoon. She could tear the whole staircase apart, but its varnish? She needed something raw and untreated, aged and dry, and she found it on her front porch, like a package that someone had mysteriously left her. Let her aunt cry about what she'd lost. Ally had her own plans for the porch, and they didn't involve this old rocking chair. In the cold of the evening she picked it up and raised it over her head. What a thrill to find it was so easy to break. What a thrill to carry it into her house in pieces. The chair was something else now. A wreck. Burning it up made the warmest fire.

We All Have Difficult Jobs

GERALD'S OFFICE DIDN'T EVEN HAVE A WINDOW. Instead, some scene in tempera on the back wall that "looked out" onto a Mediterranean seascape: cliffs, aqua ocean, tiled roofs rising up a hillside. Moored boats. It was probably the work of his wife, the faux-finisher. If there'd been a real window, he'd see the reception and waiting area for the Marquis Omaha's management office, also windowless, and it would be at least another wall Gerald would have to cut through before he got to the real outside, which from Victor's best guess would show downtown Omaha covered in slush—and not the Old Market or the riverfront. It'd be the emptied-out stretch toward the ballparks. A monochrome vista, but honest.

"It's really a super great thing for everyone," Gerald was saying. He offered up some almonds from a foil tube, which Victor declined. "You'll have more time to devote to guests with urgent and pressing needs."

"Does it know Rod Timothy?" Victor asked. "Over at Sherman's? Or does it know when Rod takes a weekend off every couple months and so to ask Carmen to find a table?"

The room felt stuffy, like a closet full of ski coats.

"The eConcierge is more of a recommendation engine, they're calling it," Gerald said. "Prints out maps, has an event calendar. Folks can still come to you if they need help, but this way they don't have to."

"I have to get back to my post," Victor said.

"Look, I'm not the bad guy here," Gerald said. "Corporate's putting one in every Marquis. Are there going to be some wrinkles? I imagine, yes, there will be wrinkles. Which is why I'm having you meet with the development team tomorrow morning."

Victor opened the door to leave. "If I have time, I'll try to stop by."

"The amount of time you spend in the bathroom?" Gerald said. "I'm sure you've got a few hours to spare."

It wasn't hours, Victor thought. Maybe an hour. And now that it was week two of the four-week low-FODMAP diet his GI doctor'd prescribed, he was hoping to get stall visits down to just twenty minutes a day, which would only mean more time to stand at his lectern in the corner of the hotel lobby and wait for people to need him. The typical scene? Men in suits with their heads bowed to little glowing screens. When he'd started at the Marquis, cordless phones were a novelty, and nobody knew how to get around or where to find a respectable escort at 9 PM on a Tuesday, but now guests took such pride in taking care of themselves. Victor worried that through no fault of his own he was becoming obsolete. As he got back to his post to start his shift, he looked for the column where Gerald'd mentioned the eConcierge would stand. They'd be facing each other across the lobby, like gunslingers sneering at high noon. Victor knew he'd have to shoot first.

The obvious thing to do was feed the development team a mess of lies. Make the machine wrong and unuseful. But when he met with Austin and Amit at Gerald's appointed time the following afternoon, he quickly found out that wasn't possible. These kids were in their twenties and had turned the dining room of the Aksarben Suite into a kind of gamer den, the table covered with six monitors and empty bags of kale chips. The first thing they asked him was what he called the female guests.

"I don't 'call them' anything," Victor said. "They're guests."

"What do you say, though?" Amit asked. "*Ma'am? Madam? Miss?*"

"And about when does a miss become a ma'am?" Austin asked.

"I thought you wanted my expertise about the town," Victor said. "Like for instance, Jojo's closes on weekdays between lunch and dinner." This was untrue. Jojo's stayed open all afternoon and relied on its happy hour business to help pay the rent, but Victor knew that if word got to its owner that the eConcierge was sending people elsewhere between 2 and 6 PM some high-up heads at the Marquis would roll.

"Nah, we've got all that," Austin said.

"Venue data was like the first thing we put in the database," Amit said, and then he turned to a keyboard, typing a few keys. "See?"

Victor looked at one of the monitors, and there was a photo of Jojo's dark stone façade and one of its empty interior. At the bottom were two large buttons: CALL JOJO'S and MAKE A RESERVATION.

"This says it's open all afternoon," Amit said. "Are you sure it closes?"

"Why am I here again?" Victor asked.

"The eConcierge works best when it feels more personal," Austin said. "We want personal Omaha touches that aren't going to work in, say, Miami or Los Angeles."

"Slang terms, superstitions, local color," said Amit.

"Superstitions?"

"In India barbers close on Tuesdays," Austin said.

"Is that true?" Amit asked.

"They say it's unlucky."

"I don't know any superstitions," Victor said. "I just know people. I know how to help them."

"Right," Austin said. "That's what we need. What are people like here?"

The people of Omaha drove to and from work and ate dinner afterward. Most but not all of them ate meat. They complained about the weather when the weather was bad. Were people any different elsewhere?

"I don't know," Victor said.

"But you're a native," Austin said. "You've got to know something about this place we can't glean from the data."

The two boys were looking at him with fingers poised on keyboards, and Victor started to feel like the whole project rested on his shoulders, which was nice to feel at forty-six. They needed something from him; he was worried it was something like people skills. But what Victor had was problem-solving skills. People came to him with fallen hems or slush-soaked Bruno Maglis, and he activated like a robot until they went away satisfied. That was his job and he loved it. These kids were putting together a problem-solver who worked in half the time, so if Victor was going to keep his job alongside the eConcierge, he'd have to get better at being a person, not a machine.

"Can I get back to you on this?" he asked.

"We're here the rest of the week," Austin said. "And don't feel bad. You've already been a big help." He pointed to a little box mounted on top of one of the monitors.

"We needed someone who looked very Nebraskan," Amit said. "For the interface. So we've captured your likeness."

"When?" asked Victor.

"This whole time," Amit said, typing away at the keyboard. There was Victor's wide, fleshy face rotating in 3D.

"Don't worry," he said. "When we're done, it'll look a lot more cartoony."

At home, Victor reheated the lobster mac and cheese Manny'd made the night before and sulked. They owned a loft five blocks from the hotel, with large south-facing windows through which snow had begun to cover the streets and sidewalks of the Old Market like sugar on a Bundt cake. His reflection in the glass looked like a dumpy ghost. Just last week a woman in an ankle-length fur stopped them outside their building and asked not Victor but big handsome Manny directions to the Marquis. She had no way of knowing what Victor did for a living, but it felt typical. People ignored him. He had a job title that made him indispensible, but strip that away and he was just one of those past-his-prime men haunting the city. "What do I have that the eConcierge doesn't?" he asked Manny in bed later.

"IBS," he said. "For starters." He was clipping his toenails right onto the bedsheet.

"Make sure you get every one of those," Victor said, sliding back from the increasing pile.

"You're also uptight. You want everything to be perfect and efficient and you get all worked up. And you need to feel useful or else you get mopey."

"You're answering pretty quickly."

Manny swept all the clippings up in his palm and tossed them in the waste bin. "You asked. I'm just being honest with you. Machines don't give a shit about being useful. They're much more Zen about all that."

Victor was used to deferring to his husband, the reporter-turned-novelist who could read you like a book, so the next day he looked up Zen online and found a meditation center out near Benson, where inside a two-story house that felt like the setting for a key party a curly-haired prairie hausfrau sat at a rickety wooden desk with a smile and thick glasses that magnified her eyeballs. "*Namaste*," she said, confusingly. Weren't these people Buddhists? Swami Pokorny, who led the session, didn't have a ponytail, but he did have that overly sonorous voice Victor knew from the poetry readings Manny sometimes dragged him to, those relentless monotones at suddenly shifting registers:

>   deep
> Nowwe'regonnatakea
>   breath.
>
>   all that
> Releaseyourmindfrom
>   bothers it.

Victor's mind felt gripped like a weapon in his hands. He couldn't let go of Gerald and the eConcierge, or Manny and his dismissive attitude toward what might be the looming end of Victor's career. What second acts exist for forty-six-year-olds in the service industry? They'd lose the loft, assuredly, and would have to live off Manny's meager salary. Would they stay together? He tried, as Swami Pokorny'd suggested, to hold a light in his heart, but all he could see was Manny in bed with someone else. That was all years ago, right before they'd been able to get married. In counseling Manny'd been penitent about his cheating, saying he'd been bored and scared but still in love with Victor, so together they decided to open up the relationship, bringing men home for both of them to share, and while Victor believed that Manny was done sleeping around on the side, he still wondered whether he'd done the right thing, tethering himself to this man so fully. After twenty minutes of long, low *om*s he felt no calmer than he did going in, and after the next session one week later he felt the same. His attitude after meditating was that other people were a distraction, some force to rid from his heart, and in wanting, John-Henry-like, to out-concierge the eConcierge he needed to figure out how to find them an allure.

He made a point never to get back to Amit and Austin, which if Gerald noticed he didn't seem to care about. One morning one of the porters didn't show up, and later word spread around the lobby that his infant daughter had died overnight. Victor spent his downtime passing a sympathy card around and getting people to pitch in to have a catering company deliver hot meals to his and his wife's house for a week. When, courageously, the porter was at his post the next morning, Victor made a little show out of delivering the card in front of the whole lobby team. Arturo nodded politely and said his thanks, but when Janet from guest services came over and set a single hand on Arturo's shoulder, he broke down and began weeping. Then everyone joined in on a group hug. Janet always wore above her cleavage a crucifix Victor thought sent mixed messages, but that morning in the lobby he was moved by the effect her simple touch had had on Arturo. Was this her Catholic god at work? He felt so naïve about these matters, having been raised nothing by agnostic parents who taught in public schools their whole careers. Every church had a flock, he knew, but in Catholic churches they drank from the same cup. That was trust. Union. Maybe he could get some for himself.

"No way in hell," Manny said when Victor brought it up over dinner that night. They were at Soy Marinero, lingering over the comped desserts which had become after fourteen years of conciering at the Marquis standard perks when they ate out—always two, because Manny refused to share. "After what those fuckers did to me, you want to go to their church?"

"I'm just asking," Victor said. "There must have been a good side. I'm looking for the good side."

"Hard to find a good side when your priest is dribbling his jizz over your fingers."

"Manny."

"I was *nine years old*," he said, shouting now. Victor was glad the place had emptied out. "You've never understood what it's been like. You claim to feel so terrible, but if that were true you wouldn't even consider this. You'd feel just as mad as I do."

He took a bite of his *tres leches* cake and then shoved the rest of the plate away, knocking over Victor's wine glass and not even moving to mop it up. Victor got to work with his napkin and thought about his next step. Manny's anger was like a wild dog they'd long ago got stuck with, one Victor still didn't like to be near. He was a large man, always had been, and Victor loved that he was big, that there was always more of him in any given room than anybody else, but a large man with Manny's temper had to be managed very carefully.

"Look, I never learned how to be close to people," Victor said.

"You're close to me. Isn't that enough?"

"I need to feel close to strangers. That's who I work with every day."

"You need religion, just read the Bible. Or, hell, read the Quran. It's better."

Victor considered this. "But I'll still be alone."

"You're not alone," Manny said. "You're with me."

Which felt only partially true. Manny's second novel was called "a moving defense of moral atheism" by one of its reviewers—though Victor didn't like it as much as his first novel, which was mostly autobiographical and thus told him all he needed to know about his husband in the dark years before they met—so no matter which church he went to he'd be going alone. If that was the case, he didn't see what the harm would be in trying one Mass. He'd be doing it for both of them. Maybe communing with strangers outside of the bedroom would bring the two closer together.

One Sunday morning he took a cab out to St. Cecilia so Manny wouldn't find the car missing. He paid cash. It was easy. All of Omaha was asleep, it seemed, the parking lot half empty, dawn just breaking, the air crisp and prickly. St. Cecilia rose up like a space shuttle he was about to board, and inside, the hall was colorful and full of shadows. Up around the altar were a series of carved guys, some carrying little totemic objects; Victor couldn't imagine ever being Catholic enough to know who was who and what to ask them for. Their faces were so long, they looked to him like a set of advertisements for despair. He took a far pew and tried to look approachable. Right at nine thirty, every person in the church stood up as a salt-and-pepper-haired man in white robes stepped to the podium. Victor stood up, too.

"In the name of the Father and of the Son and of the Holy Spirit," he said, crossing himself as others did the same. "Today the diocese has set aside in remembrance of unborn children, and so we give our Mass in honor of those gentle warriors." He lifted his hands and looked up to the bright yellow ceiling. "Lord God, you created us in our mothers' wombs, and so we pray for the strength to carry that loving care forward to those who do not have a voice."

Victor's heart sank. Maybe Manny was right about Catholics. This priest had a soft face on a hard, withering body, and given what he knew of priests it was hard for Victor to trust him. Soon everyone sat, and so he sat, and when, later, they stood again, he too again stood. This hokey-pokey raised his woeful spirits. He also liked the prayer that soon came: "Lord God, we pray for those seeking help and guidance. We pray for Loreen Hottovy as she recovers from knee surgery, and I continue to pray for my brother, Bud, who is dying from cancer."

Everyone in the church then spoke together: "Lord, hear our prayer."

"We pray for justice and peace for the unemployed and for the homeless."

"Lord, hear our prayer."

Then a couple of tiny old Latin women spoke up with the names of other people in need, but he couldn't hear what they were supposed to be praying for. Still, he repeated it: *Lord, hear our prayer.* Afterward, the priest invited everyone to wish peace on their fellow congregants, and a round man in overalls turned around, looked Victor in the eye, and offered his hand.

"Peace be with you," he said.

"Thanks," Victor said, taking his hand. "Er, you too."

It felt like what being welcomed into a cult must've felt like. And for two days afterward, toilet trips for Victor were as carefree as tossing his keys on the entrance table. Christ's glory! He went back the next Sunday and the next, and then another month of Sundays, each time telling Manny some small falseness about work, relieved to find that there was a rotation of priests who didn't stalk the pulpit so much as embrace it warmly. He knew about Leviticus and stoning people, and he'd been told plenty of times that God hated fags, but if that were true no one here was mentioning it. Instead it was all *judge not that ye be not judged* and *consider the lilies.* Victor hated lilies, but that was okay. The lily wasn't going to change to please him, was the point. He stood tall when called to, and he knelt on the little red-velvet curb. He shook all the hands he could reach. He didn't line up for communion, because it didn't feel respectful, but at work he started asking guests their names and giving his. The eConcierge was installed in April, and in testing it out Victor saw that the Jeevesy character on the screen had been dressed in a tuxedo, whereas Victor'd always had to furnish his own suits, and dry-clean them. The guy looked just like Victor, too, but nicer.

One afternoon Gerald summoned him again to his office. He was in workout gear doing dips off the edge of the sofa, leaving Victor nowhere to sit. The fake little window was gone. "What happened to your wall?" Victor asked.

"That fucking thing?" Gerald said, between breaths. He was at least five years older than Victor, and yet his triceps stretched the sleeves of his T-shirt every time his ass neared the floor. "It was depressing. I had maintenance paint over it."

"Didn't your wife make it?" Victor asked.

"It wasn't fitting the office of a manager," he said.

Victor tried to see Gerald as Gerald saw himself, but that was hard to do when just last week he'd forbidden porters to ride in the main elevators unless they were escorting a guest or her luggage. They now had to share the single service elevator with housekeeping and room service. Never mind it was harder to get enough baggage carts, Gerald now had some level of decorum nobody'd ever asked for.

"I want to talk about why you're taking so many Sunday mornings off," he said. "Is it a church thing?"

Victor laughed. "Do I look like a God-fearing man?"

"You look like you're abusing your seniority," Gerald said, moving on to squats by his desk. "How busy this place gets with checkouts? I can't have my top concierge gone. Whatever's going on, cut it out, or we're going to have to let you go."

"We?" he asked. "You and the crown?"

"I'm serious, Vic. You're on rocky ground here."

St. Cecilia had evening masses on Saturdays and Wednesdays, and while it was rare for Victor to have to work evenings, it was easy telling Manny he had to. He wasn't used to lying, but Manny's suspicions over the last few weeks had become sudden land mines Victor had to hotfoot around. What happened to all the church stuff, he asked out on the patio at Rod Timothy's divorce party. Had Victor just given up on all that? Victor said he'd visited one church—Unitarian—but that it was too singsongy and he didn't go back. "They had a banjo player with a topknot you would've been all over," he added, and Manny only shrugged and slugged more of his beer. Actually, Victor couldn't remember the last time they'd brought somebody home with them. Sitting in Mass, eyes closed in prayer, he took all he heard about love and let it fill him like a kind of food he'd been missing, his body made whole from his head to his heart to his bowels. With such holy energy coursing through him twice a week now, he'd come home, seek Manny out like a target, and they'd maul each other like a pair of nervous marines. When they weren't fucking they'd be on the couch in the TV room, Victor trying always to get somehow closer inside Manny's warm embrace. It was nothing Victor understood, and nothing he wanted to mess up, and he thanked God for it.

He told himself he'd tell Manny the truth, eventually, convincing him that the church had given them all this. The church of his family. Until then, he went to work and did the work of the Lord. One morning a barrage of customer demands came at the same hour, and he breathed slowly and deeply and faced it like a harlot buried to her neck. One guest needed advice on whether the solid navy or red-and-black repp tie would give him a better shot at the job interview he was almost late for. Another's shoelace snapped. A French couple had a meeting with a mediator and couldn't find a daytime sitter for their seven-year-old. These were eConciergeable problems Old Victor would delegate and solve with the least amount of friction, but wasn't friction the stuff of life? People became persons only when you ran into them, sometimes physically, so that morning New Victor not only chose the more youthful repp tie, but he also led the young man into the men's room to four-in-hand it into the perfect dimpled knot. He didn't call a taxi for the second guest to hoof it over to the shoe repair place on Dodge, he gave that man his own shoelace, close enough of a match. And he didn't ask one of the servers at the adjacent Prairie Lake Grill to watch the seven-year-old on her lunch break, he did it himself, finding in the lost-and-found a coloring book and some crayons and sitting with the boy in a far corner of the restaurant, coloring together. *I have,* Victor thought, *a difficult job,* but there was glory—wasn't there?—in its difficulty, and here he was, rising up to face it.

Why hadn't Victor found religion sooner? Or why hadn't it found him? He felt one warm evening in mid-May that it was time to step out from whatever he might've been hiding behind, and at Mass when his favorite priest—the one with the big wagging eyebrows—began the preparation of the Eucharist, he felt his gut tighten and the fire in his heart get hotter. He would, he decided, stand in line and receive for the first time the holy host. It would be the final cure. He got up and filed down the row with his fellow congregants, and the corner of his eye was caught by a large figure standing in the back of the room. Manny. Victor stopped his walk. His pewmate stumbled into the back of him. He watched Manny shake his head and walk out of the church.

In the choice between host and husband, he ran after the husband. Months later, he'd remember how it felt to make that decision instinctively.

Manny was opening the car door by the time he caught up with him. "I don't want to hear it," he said. "Whatever you have to say."

"I've been meaning to tell you," Victor said. "It's been helping. My IBS, and at home. Haven't we—"

"I want you to listen to me very carefully," Manny said, closing the door so there was now nothing between them. "My priest raped me. My Catholic priest. When we started getting serious I was so afraid to tell you. I was sure you'd break up with me. I know it doesn't make sense, but I felt dirty. I felt like a stupid victim and I thought you'd feel—"

"Well, now we're even," Victor said, pleased to find that the fire in his heart hadn't left him.

"What?"

"Now we're even."

"What the fuck does that mean?"

"Now we've both cheated on each other," he said, and he walked off to call a cab.

He was relieved that he didn't have to lie to Manny anymore. Maybe they'd turned a corner in their marriage. Maybe they could start going to Mass together. Manny would see that the eyebrow priest was different, that the faith was big enough to welcome him back. Not that they actually talked about this. That night Victor'd come home to find the bedroom door locked, and for the next few nights he made his bed on the couch, where he'd lie awake for hours listening to the sounds of Omaha waft up through the open windows. He imagined all the couples hand in hand exiting bars he knew the owners of. Smoking boys up against the wall of the danceclub. That guy with the little accordion getting tips in his bowler. He prayed every night for God to help Manny come around.

Just after Memorial Day, Gerald called Victor into his office and said he had some bad news. "You and I been having problems for some time now, haven't we?" he asked.

"I've been giving my best to the hotel," Victor said. "I've actually been falling in love with my job all over again."

"Well, I see us having problems for some time to come. You've been skipping out on Sundays, when I need you most."

"I put an end to that after we last talked."

"And customer feedback on the eConcierge is outstanding, despite the fact that you never bothered to help Austin and Amit like I'd asked you to. It's going far better than we'd expected. People prefer the kiosk, and our online user reviews are up. In the end, it's a money issue. This economy, you see."

Victor stared at him. "What about it?"

"Well," he said, "you know," he said, and shrugged.

Victor was given two months' severance and ten thousand MarqPerq Points to spend at any Echelon Family hotel in the world, which by his estimate would garner one night's stay at a golf resort in Tampa. Manny hated golf; in a book he called it "Jarts for the greedy and diseased." At home, Victor felt useless. His forty-seventh birthday came and went without fanfare. Manny had warmed enough to him to make a dry cake he kept beating himself up about, but Victor remained each night on the couch. He knew he was not his job, but without that job and without a partner to talk to, he didn't know who was left. Who was he supposed to be? A butler? A priest? The only thing that made him feel like a living human and not some ghost haunting the loft was that St. Cecilia had a daily Mass at 7 AM, and so he was able to wake early, dress himself nice, and arrive on time in some large public place where people like him wanted help with the day. He felt good to be among the truly penitent, the purest in their faith. One Asian woman came in every morning whispering, "Jesus, Jesus, Jesus, Jesus," as she walked from the holy water font to the statue of St. Cecilia to the side chapel, where she'd light a candle in a blue glass cup and then take her seat, the whole time keeping up with "Jesus, Jesus," as though his very name were the air she breathed. She came alone and sat alone and every morning had a list of people the congregants asked the Lord to hear their prayers for. Victor watched her with sorry eyes. He wanted to be her brother.

If there was a bright side in his life it was the money he was saving on cab fare. Manny never needed the car so early in the morning. One day he was in the kitchen drinking coffee when Victor came back from a Mass that had featured the adulteress and casting first stones. Manny asked him how he was feeling and Victor said he was feeling humble but good about the sin in his life. "We all have it," he said.

Manny started rubbing at his eyes, which after eleven years Victor knew he did when frustrated, but what did he have to be frustrated about? He had a job.

"When are you going to stop?" Manny asked.

"Stop what?" Victor hung his suit jacket on the edge of a kitchen chair and started unloosing his tie.

"This stupid journey you're on," Manny said. "This whole fucking thing. You don't even see it as a betrayal, and now you're going every day. Do you feel better, doing this to me?"

"I'm doing it for me."

"And what has it left you with? What do you have now?"

"I have you," Victor said.

"You won't," Manny said. "Not if you keep this up."

One thing he'd learned was that if he was made in God's image, it meant there was a part of God inside him, and so he'd never be alone.

Victor kicked off his shoes and lay down on the sofa. "You don't get to tell me what to do," he said. There was nothing good on TV that early in the morning, but he kept flipping through the channels, certain he'd find something.

The morning Manny moved out Victor decided to stand in line for communion. This time for keeps. He made his slow way to the front of the room, past the pew ends carved to look like lilies, past the faces of Mary and Joseph rendered in stained glass, and right up to the statuette of Jesus on the cross. There he opened his mouth for his favorite priest. So what if the body was tasteless and the blood watered thin? Outside, the world felt tilted off its axis and Victor was no longer in control.

If You Need Me I'll Be Over There

WOULD YOU RISK YOUR LIFE TO SAVE MINE? DEAN ASKS, shutting off the car. Think about it, before you answer yes. Imagine a scenario.

You want me to do this now? I ask, digging through the glovebox for the mints. We've been silent the whole drive over—comfortably, I've thought—but now I'm in some guessing game. What's on my husband's mind? That morning I'd joined him in the shower and tried to get something started between us, but he was all business with the soap bar. Are you sure we have to go? I said, drawing him closer.

We're the godparents, Christopher.

Well, *you're* the godparent really, I said. I'm just his husband. That's when he'd gone quiet. It fit the mood of the day. Driving out here to Castle Shannon was like going into an ever-danker thicket, the trees all stripped bare, the sky a low plaster ceiling I felt I could reach through the sunroof and scrape my palm on.

Just take some time, he says now, getting out of the car. I watch him slouch by the door, hefting his pants. His suit looks like it's holding him up. I probably look the same in mine. We've grown old and outward. Unbuckling my seatbelt I see I've spilled coffee on my shirtbelly.

Marlon Brando, I remember, was also a fat godfather.

The church is a mid-century industrial block in buttery brick. We've parked at the far end of a long, thin lot and we hustle toward what might be a service entrance. We're late. Your hair looks nice today, I say trailing him, trying to find some affirming words. It's true: he's been growing it out this last year and it's got some bounce to it and catches the morning's low sun as we jog up the stairs.

No answer.

I hit the men's room to see about the stain on my shirt and to piss out whatever I can before the ceremony starts. In the mirror I'm trying to skew my tie just so when the door opens and Dean's dad, Sal, walks in.

Buddy, good, you boys made it, he says. His hand in mine feels skeletal and light. His walk over to the urinal, one of those greyed porcelain recesses that falls to the floor, is slacked and shuffling, like a marionette. Catelynn's got a spiderbite, you hear?

Oh *no.*

He's looking me in the eye as he pisses. On her thigh somewhere. Been screaming all morning. He starts tugging at himself and I turn to the mirror to check my teeth even though I haven't eaten yet this morning. Sal joins me at the sinks. I hear crying from somewhere very far away. Never thought I'd be a granddad, he says, pulling a hanky from his pants pocket. Each one feels like another nail in the coffin. 'Course I love them all.

Let's hope this is the last one, then.

He looks at me. You and Dean?

If we adopted tomorrow, I'd be fifty-eight when our kid graduated from high school, and what kind of age is that for a father?

Not likely, I say.

Sal hawks a wad of phlegm into the sink. Enjoy your freedom, son.

Have we been? The only debt we have is the mortgage, plus a couple thousand left on my student loans. We've been able to buy anything we need, for the most part. Dean's paid for cars in cash. Is that freedom? I married him to get on his benefits, but I wanted to be married to him because I could see he'd be the kind of man who'd pay cash for cars. Used cars, but still: dependable. Whenever I ask why he wanted to be married to me, he jokes about my "wide birthing hips," so it remains a mystery. Sometimes, I wonder: does he even like me? At work, there's a new producer heading up the weekend evening news who wears a suit every day, cufflinks and all. Last week in the editing room he told me he was nervous about his ten-year reunion this summer. Ten years out of high school. He's got two kids and a house in Sewickley. I work late cutting news footage or custom ads for Pizzaburgh and Don Putski Ford. I have a husband and a house on the North Side. We haven't had a kid, because we haven't felt ready, so now we're free to have forty more years of just each other.

I follow Sal down two long hallways stretched with linoleum and low fluorescents overhead, and we join Dean and the rest of the Hubbards in front of a closed set of doors. The screaming's stopped, little Catelynn in just a diaper, sloppily, and silenced for the moment by a pacifier. Jillian, holding her, looks tired but gorgeous, like a senator's wife, and Brandon's dressed like a guy on a game show: gold tie on black shirt. All here, finally? the priest asks. He's wearing long white robes and a scowl aimed at me, and his beard is neat but urgently orange, like a holy flame he seems to breathe. He has a series of questions for the parents that I tune out. I'd given the script Brandon emailed me last week a quick skim and saw that my job was to keep answering in the affirmative.

What do you ask of God's church? says the priest.

Eternal life, say Jillian and Brandon.

And where are the godparents?

Dean puts an arm around my back and guides us closer. The priest looks at us like we're two mimes. Are you ready to help the parents of this child in their duty as Christians?

Dean says, We are, and I look at him and say, Are we? There's a chuckle among the Hubbards, and I turn to the priest. Sorry. Is it okay if I'm not technically a Christian?

There are worse sins, my son, he says, which gets him an even bigger laugh even though I'm clearly his elder.

Organ music accompanies our walk to a back corner of the room. I'm second in line, with Dean. Potted palm fronds all around the altar make it look like the set of a Robinson Crusoe passion play. Firebeard leads us around a wide low dais on which there's a kind of kiddie pool made of old tile, with an aqua blue cross inlaid at the bottom. We stand opposite Jillian and Brandon, the priest facing out between us at the twenty-some family members who've gathered to watch this little girl get Catholicked.

The hymn ends and the priest opens his Bible and starts to read something *thou*ful and strung with *and*s. I hear, Except a man be born again, he cannot see the kingdom of God, and I think: *Oh, here we go.*

I move to take Dean's hand but he turns to me and shakes his head. Once, I asked him if we had a son whether we'd circumcise him. Dean said yes pretty quickly. I don't want him feeling like he's different from his fathers, he said, as though it'd been so destructive to us two. Having been so long in the closet I know how feeling different can eat nightly at a part of you, until you can feel this cold cavern someplace you hope's not your heart. Still, I wouldn't give it up. That moment you call yourself out and step into a new role you don't yet understand, that's a rebirth worth much more than the kingdom of God. Catelynn, here, is being born again so quickly, why didn't they just kill two birds and birth the girl right into the baptismal font?

I feel sorry for her, which is an interesting feeling to have for a perfect stranger. Then again, she may be the closest I get to being a parent, and Jarem's being sterile means that whatever amounts to the May line ends with me, not that I know much about those people. How many of them died at forty, and how many of those died happy? Did they have someone they called The Love of Their Life? Did he pay for horse buggies in cash?

I try to stay focused on the ceremony, but everyone keeps repeating Lord, hear our prayer and I feel mostly ornamental. I'm the only non-Catholic here. Well, and Catelynn. There's a woman in the front of the crowd whose eyes are shut tight against the world and who clutches in two hands a crucifix the size of a ninja star. Maybe she's an aunt or great-aunt. She's wearing dark spangled denim and I can see that her fly is down.

I check and, wouldn't you know it, so is mine.

Then the priest starts talking about evil. We pray for this child: set her free from original sin and make her a temple of your glory. We ask this through Christ our Lord. He reaches over to a tray draped in white cloth and grabs a small vial, which he calls the oil (so it sounds to me) of catty humans. I raise my hand.

Sorry, I say. What is it called?

All eyes on me and the priest repeats it.

Can you spell that? I ask. Just curious.

I look at Dean and he's got his eyes closed.

C-a-t, e-c-h, u-m, e-n-s, says the priest, and he adds that back in the time of Jesus it was put on the breastplates of soldiers so that spears and arrows would find little purchase. Lucky girl. Would that I had such armor from birth. The priest dabs some on his finger and makes the sign of the cross on Catelynn's bare chest, and like that the pacifier falls to the floor and her screams reverberate off the walls of this wide room. Jillian sighs and fobs the baby off on Brandon, and some of the older women in the room come over to try to soothe and coo. It's some time before we're able to continue.

Dean leans in to me. I can't believe you interrupted the service.

It's not like he was channeling the Holy Ghost, I say. I'm trying to be fully invested.

This isn't about you, he says.

Aren't I the godfather?

Then he says, Why do you always have to embarrass me? and my immediate instinct is to leave, to go wait in the car and not think about his stupid question. How do I know he would risk his life for me? I look for the clearest escape, but Catelynn's stopped her crying and it's clear we have to start speaking again. The priest asks us, Do you reject Satan as the symbol of darkness and evil? and I relax and start grinning. We've come to the good part, the one I remember. I say my *I do*s like Michael Corleone: solemnly and full of responsibility, my mind on guns, blood, and carnage.

After all the song and dance it's time to actually douse the girl, but again Catelynn's squirmy and screaming, ruining all the photos that relatives are holding tablets up to capture. Brandon hands her back to Jillian but this only makes her cry harder. Let's just blow through it, she yells. Sorry, everyone. It's been a long morning.

My therapist says the way to work through anger is to play a violent cartoon in your head, so I take a moment to tackle Dean and hold him under the font's holy water until he cries uncle. I see him soaked, his hair stringy and dripping. I pull his fly down. Then I feel bad, because I want him to look nice in front of his family. Ten years together and I can't think of a single time he's ever embarrassed me. I've leaned on him like a hip I prefer. How could I ever return the favor?

I step up to the font and face the priest. Can I try? I ask, pointing at Catelynn. Is it okay?

Of course, he says, and Jillian holds the child out to me.

I take Catelynn and hold her tightly to my chest and her little feet kick at my big stained belly. I say Shh and bounce her until they stop. The priest directs me to bring her down to the water and I hold her there, standing. Her diaper soaks, but she just stares at me with enormous eyes. Flashbulbs fire in the air around us. *How hard your life is going to be*, I want to tell her. *How many days you're going to have to fill in ways that don't lead you to despair*. I am trying to be in this moment, to hold on to it before the priest pours over her head the water he's lifted in the air. I stare back at Catelynn, but I can see the people around me, this family that's not really mine but mine for the asking. And I see Dean. And I can see he's smiling. I hope he's proud of me for this. If he's the love of my life—who else?—then what kind of life would I be left to live without him? That's a string of days I couldn't bear, so of course I'd risk my life to save his. It'd be my last selfish act. That I might take the bullet, or the mugger's blade. That I might serve up my neck for the charging pitbull and fall so my husband can stand. That I might find myself at the end of my days and bathed, at last, in light.

Reading Group Guide

1. Why is the title story split up in three parts? What effect does it have that might be lost if it were one cohesive story?

2. Other than the title trilogy, these are not linked stories. Do they make a kind of progression, start to finish? If so, what kind, or if not, why not?

3. Religious themes pop up in a number of the stories, with some characters seeking spirituality and others shunning it. How do their attitudes toward faith help or hinder their journeys?

4. Twice, the author (male) writes from the first-person point of view of female characters. To what extent is this "okay" or "not okay," and how does the rendering of Erica in "Pamela" and Ginny in "Little Fingers" compare to, say, that of the men in the collection?

5. Several of the protagonists in the book are gay. What gay heroes can you think of from popular fiction? What kinds of stories have we told about gay men, and how do these compare?

6. Is coming out as gay a kind of rebirth? Would these characters agree with you? Which ones?

7. Were any of the protagonists unlikeable? Why? What kept you reading, or kept you *from* reading?

8. These stories rely chiefly on first-person narrators: "*My* father bought *me* a car." What kind of limitations come with such a point of view? Why do these people need to confess, and what, if anything, are they hiding?

9. At the end of "An Uneven House," the point of view shifts from the husband to the wife. Why does she get to end things? Whose story is this?

10. Many of the stories concern people's jobs. To what extent are these characters defined by their occupations, and to what extent do they resist such classification?

11. These stories are set on the East Coast, the West Coast, and places in between. How does place influence the people who live there? Could these stories be set anywhere? If not, why not? And if so, what kind of America is this?

12. Recall Buddy's therapist's notion on families: we have to define ourselves in terms of others before we know who we want to become. Was this true for you? How is it true—or not—for Buddy? And the other characters?

13. Infertility and infidelity are recurring themes. Why is sex so troublesome for these characters? What are they missing in their lives, or within themselves, that might help?

14. Victor's story ends after he's lost his job and his husband, but also after he's found God and faith. How is this a happy ending for him? What about for you? If there's a difference, what might that signify?

15. Could any of these stories be made into a movie? If so, how? If not, why not?

DAVE MADDEN is the author of *The Authentic Animal: Inside the Odd and Obsessive World of Taxidermy*. His shorter work has appeared in *Harper's, Prairie Schooner, Indiana Review, The Normal School*, and elsewhere. He is the recipient of a Sherwood Anderson Award in fiction, a Bernard De Voto Fellowship at the Bread Loaf Writers' Conference, and a Tennessee Williams Scholarship at the Sewanee Writers' Conference. He teaches in the MFA program at the University of San Francisco.

Printed and bound by CPI Group (UK) Ltd, Croydon, CR0 4YY

13/04/2025

14656551-0001